PUSHKIN PRESS CLASSICS

CHANGE
YOUR
LIFE

ESSENTIAL POEMS

T0038166

CHANGE YOUR LIFE

ESSENTIAL POEMS

RAINER MARIA RILKE

SELECTED, TRANSLATED,
AND INTRODUCED
BY MARTYN CRUCEFIX

PUSHKIN PRESS CLASSICS

Pushkin Press
Somerset House, Strand
London WC2R 1LA

English translation © 2024 Martyn Crucefix

This selection and translation first published by Pushkin Press in 2024

1 3 5 7 9 8 6 4 2

ISBN 13: 978-1-78227-858-0

Designed and typeset by Tetragon, London
Printed and bound in the United Kingdom by Clays Ltd, Elcograf S.p.A.

www.pushkinpress.com

The rain running its cold fingers
down our windows, unseeing;
we lean back in deep armchairs
to listen, as if the quiet hours
dripped from a weary mill all evening.

Then Lou speaks. Our souls incline
one to another. Even cut flowers
in the window nod their utmost bloom,
and we are utterly at home,
here, in this tranquil, white house.

'To Celebrate You', unpublished, 1898?

The transformed speaks only to those who let go. All
who cling on choke

Unpublished notebook entry, 1917

Rose, oh sheer contradiction, joy,
being no one's sleep beneath so many
lids.

Epitaph, composed by Rilke for himself,
27th October 1925

*for Debra Allbery—for first
pointing me towards Rilke*

*for Mario Petrucci—for
encouraging me to keep going*

CONTENTS

ACKNOWLEDGEMENTS

Some of these translations (or earlier versions of them) have appeared with the following journals and websites: *Acumen*, *Agenda*, *Asymptote*, *Caduceus Journal*, *Long Poem Magazine*, *Magma*, *Modern Poetry in Translation*, *New Welsh Review*, *Other Poetry*, *The Fortnightly Review*, *Trespass*.

Sonnets to Orpheus, I 24 was first broadcast on BBC Radio 3 in March 2011 in the Sunday Feature entitled 'Amongst the Ranks of the Angels: Rainer Maria Rilke'. The producer was Julian May.

I am very grateful to all at Pushkin Press, especially Adam Freudenheim and Rory Williamson, for the opportunity to put this book together. Thanks are also due to Will Stone for originally and so generously offering to throw my hat into the ring and to Linden Lawson for her indefatigable eye for detail.

I am indebted to the Royal Literary Fund for awarding me fellowships at the British Library and the School of Advanced Studies, University of London, which enabled me to encourage the writing of others in a variety of forms as well as spend time working on these translations of Rilke.

The selections of my translations from *Duino Elegies* and *Sonnets to Orpheus* are slightly revised versions of those originally published by (and still in print with) Enitharmon Press in 2006 and 2012 respectively. In those publications, I thanked Stephen Stuart-Smith (and thank him again here for his kind permission to reprint). The *Duino Elegies* translation, in particular, was dedicated to Nick and Candy and all the Fine Arts people of the late 1990s.

There is no end to the particular debt I owe to two genuine Germanists: David Constantine and Karen Leeder. Other debts of conversation, consolation, casual chats and general encouragement remain due to Debra Allbery, Neil Curry, Hilary Davies, Clive Eastwood, Sue Hubbard, Valerie Jack, Joan Michelson, Mario Petrucci, Denis Timm, Tim Turner, James Wykes and Aprilia Zank.

INTRODUCTION

In Moscow, in May 1900, the Russian writer Sofia Schill observed 'a thin young man of middle height wearing a queer felt hat and a jacket covered in pockets. [He was] as fair of skin as a girl; his nose and oval face were elongated; his large pale eyes gazed with the clarity of an infant's... Nothing could have become him more than his little brown goatee.'[1] This was the twenty-five-year-old Rainer Maria Rilke, during his second visit to Russia. At this point he had already published several books of poetry, but would later dismiss them as consisting of mere 'cloudiness'. Twenty-six years on, the great Russian poet Marina Tsvetaeva would write to Rilke, praising him and his work as constituting a veritable 'topography of the soul'; in 1932, she set him up as nothing less than a 'counterpoise' to the accumulating horrors of the early twentieth century: 'The earth will be forgiven for our times for the sake of Rilke, who lived in them. He could have been born only in our times because he is their opposite, because he is essential, because he is an antidote. That is what makes him our contemporary.'[2]

The poetry felt to justify elevating this thin young man to near-divine status is comprehensively traced in this new selection and translation of Rilke's essential poetry. His reputation is that of a 'pure' poet, one whose sole aim was to express the nature of the world (both inward and outward) in evocative, lambent, musical language. Yet his life project was a more broad, passionate exploration of our loss of and potential recovery of wholeness of being. He writes of how we create deities from the 'unwieldy and ungraspable forces' of our own inner life which we then place 'outside us'.[3] As we forget the origins of these false gods, they come to exert a malign influence upon us. He felt the same sleight of perception had also been performed in our relationship with death so that, once externalized and similarly alienated, we come to see it as the contradiction, the adversary of all we love, of all we narrowly define by the term 'life'.

Hence, we find ourselves living lives that are alienated and baffled, with our perceptions cramped and distorted by preconceptions. Rilke's work hinges on his rejection of the illusory transcendent, his embracing of death as part of life itself and his consequent praising of the resultant, renovated, more expansive notion of our being in the world. Crucially, the language we use to describe and understand our lives does not escape suspicion: it too can be a source of delusion. So Rilke's extraordinary poetic skills are progressively deployed as no mere vehicle of expression: his vision of the truth could not be articulated through conventional language but only as song: 'Oh, Orpheus singing! Oh, tall tree in the ear!'

Rilke was born René Karl Wilhelm Johann Josef Maria Rilke in Prague in 1875. His father was a stolid, occasionally rough soldier-turned-railway-worker while his mother aspired socially and spiritually, with an almost manic devotion to the forms of Catholicism. His mother's faith spurred the young man's wariness of orthodox religion as well as his lifelong commitment to truth and honesty. She seems to have found some consolation in dressing her son in girl's clothing. At the age of ten, the father's influence packed him off to military school, but this proved an unmitigated disaster. Back in Prague, the young René, emerging from what he called an 'unachieved childhood', fell variously in love and took refuge in a facility for writing unremarkable poems, publishing collections almost annually through the mid-1890s.

The most important encounter of his life, in May 1897, was with the thirty-seven-year-old Lou Andreas-Salomé, already well known in German modernist circles for her philosophical and critical writings, her fiction and a book about her friendship with Friedrich Nietzsche. Lou transformed her lover's handwriting, and his name (to Rainer). Rilke wrote how, under her influence, the world 'lost its cloudiness for me, this fluid forming and sur-rendering of itself, which was the manner and poverty of my first verses; [. . .] I learnt a simplicity [. . .] I gained the maturity to speak of simple things'.[4] He also came to sense the danger posed by what he called 'the interpreted world'. By this he meant a world view shorn of all mystery (the one, of course, that most of us inhabit most of the time). Language, consequently, becomes narrowly instrumental, merely utilitarian, rather than capable of evoking the full mysterious truth, the oneness of being.

It was with Lou that Rilke travelled twice to Russia. There, he seems to have hoped to find a country living closer to Nature, a people who had not yet exhausted the wealth of their spiritual resources. These Russian experiences bore fruit in the poems he wrote in 1899 that became *The Book of Monastic Life*. In some, he adopts the persona of a Russian icon painter who, in the opening poem, hears the monastery bell ringing:

There! The hour inclines and stirs me awake
with its clear, metallic blow

[...]

I love all things—there is nothing too small,
but boldly I paint it on gold

Over the next five years, Rilke added two more collections of poems to *Monastic Life* (*The Book of Pilgrimage* [1901] and *The Book of Poverty and Death* [1903]), eventually publishing the whole in 1905 as *The Book of Hours*. Without doubt, this is Rilke's first really significant work. By the end of his life, the *Hours* had outsold the now far more acclaimed *New Poems* twofold.

However, after their second Russian sojourn, Lou brought their relationship to an end and Rilke spent time at an artists' community in Worpswede, in northern Germany, where he seems to have fallen in love with two women artists. Paula Becker eventually married Otto Modersohn and she died soon after giving birth to her child. Rilke's 1909 poem 'Requiem for a Friend' is his moving meditation on her fate. In the end, it was Clara Westhoff whom Rilke married, and the couple had a daughter, Ruth. But married life, with its compromises and the responsibilities of parenthood, was not Rilke's style. It was not long before he set off on the hard road of his chosen vocation, a solitary, artistic pilgrimage.

By 1902 he was working alone in Paris, a city which heavily influenced the third section of *The Book of Hours*, with its portraits of urban poverty, as well as his only novel, *The Notebooks of Malte*

Laurids Brigge. It was also the opportunity to observe Auguste Rodin, the great sculptor, that drew him to the French capital. Rilke's progress towards a poetic style that cultivated the 'earthly', the world of 'things', was well under way and, astonishingly, even as the *Hours* was being completed, he had also been writing the poems collected in 1902 as *The Book of Images*. Many of these poems still look back to conventionally religious subjects, but others foreshadow the *New Poems* in their steady, 'earthly', observations:

> The evening is slowly changing its clothes,
> held for it by a rim of ancient trees;
> you watch: and the earth, growing distant, moves,
> this slipping from you, this lifted to the skies;

Rodin's methods of closely observing the real world fascinated Rilke and, in parallel, he became a more self-conscious labourer in the German language. In a poem like 'The Panther', the fruits of a more compact diction, a more supple syntax, and a lexis of more precise everyday words can be seen:

> The lithe, smooth steps of his powerful gait
> that, within the smallest of circles, spins round,
> is like a dance of power about a point
> at which an immense will stands, stunned.

The two volumes of *New Poems* contain works that can be held up as examples of what Rilke termed 'art-things'. He wrote to Lou: 'The thing is definite, the art-thing must be even more definite; removed from all accident, removed from ambiguity, released from time and given to space.'[5] Roaming through Paris (including the city zoo and the Bois de Boulogne), Rilke found subjects in a gazelle, parrots, a swan, flowers, a burned-out house, fountains and other art objects. The *New Poems* are not merely studiedly objective (as is often said), nor are they subjective, but complicatedly both at once. Gazing at Rodin's work, Rilke began to understand that a sculpture's surface 'consisted of an infinite number of encounters of light with the object [...] and there were such places of encounter without end, and none where something was not happening. There was no emptiness.'[6] In a Rodin sculpture—as he wished for in his own poetry—Rilke saw that 'no part of the body was insignificant or slight: it lived'.[7] This recalls the description of the surface of the 'Archaic Torso of Apollo', upon which, as an act of perception and an implied imperative, 'there is no place / that does not see you. You must change your life.'

Rilke published almost nothing for a little over a decade following the appearance of the second volume of *New Poems*. In fact, though he seems to have felt it *was* a period of drought (and discussed it as such often in his letters), poems were being written and the years between 1910 and 1922 were also filled with much reading (of Friedrich Hölderlin especially) and translation work. The limits of an orientation towards the visual arts—as learnt at Worpswede, alongside Rodin, and powerfully deployed in the *New Poems*—are scrutinized, for example, in the poem 'Turning Point':

> For there is, you see, a limit to looking.
> And the world, so looked-upon,
> wants to flourish in love.

20

What is now required, the poem implies, in addition to mere observation, is what he calls 'heart-work', a more conscious focus on the self-transformative, affective possibilities of the work of noticing.

The long-nurtured fruits of these cumulative lessons in observation, feeling, a provisional vision of life, poetic diction, and syntax are what burst from Rilke years later at Muzot. Much has been written about the inspired 'hurricane of the heart and mind' that resulted in the completion of both the *Duino Elegies* and the *Sonnets to Orpheus* in a few weeks of February 1922. The *Duino* poems are not elegies in any formal or traditional sense, but they dramatize the kind of loss that had always been Rilke's subject: the necessary loss of our necessary preconceptions about the world, so that we can (if only passingly) experience with truth and honesty its ultimate nature as a wholeness of being. The angels who make brief appearances stand for all that we are not (yet might briefly glimpse). The lack of self-consciousness Rilke perceives in natural creatures—their capacity to see the Open without the screens of self-conscious reflection—proves to be an alternative way of critiquing the way we live. Attending to the natural world, to the earthly, enables us to gain greater distance from 'interpretation'—the conceptual world—until, as the seventh Duino poem proclaims: 'Simply being here is glorious!'

Applying lessons learnt from his predecessor, Hölderlin, Rilke understood that the only chance of preserving the sense of such glory is to be sure that no single particular interpretation of experience becomes fixed, is not taken as solely valid. The language of poetry itself becomes a way of circumventing interpretation, attaching ourselves to things, going out to the world, engaging ourselves with it, all the while retaining a sense of its inevitable provisionality. We are, then, to eschew the 'wooing' of angels, for the truth is 'my call is always filled with leaving and against / such a powerful current [angels] cannot advance'. As the ninth elegy declares, '*Here* is the time for what can be *said*—here its home.' The final poem, with its strange allegorical landscapes and personages, argues that '*here*' must also encompass human death. Rilke wrote to his Polish translator: 'Affirmation of *life-AND-death* appears as one in the "Elegies"... we must try to achieve the fullest consciousness of our existence, which is at home in both unbounded realms, inexhaustibly nourished by both.'[8]

Alongside what Rilke called the 'gigantic white canvas' of the *Duino Elegies* came the 'little rust-coloured sail' of the Orphic songs of the *Sonnets to Orpheus*.[9] Rilke's Eurydice was Vera Ouckama Knoop. In Munich, before the war, she had been a playmate of his own now neglected daughter. She was beautiful, a dancer, and attracted much attention through the 'art of movement and transformation which was innate in her body and spirit'.[10] She abandoned dance as she reached her teens and was found to be suffering from leukaemia (the same illness that would end Rilke's life). Vera's artistic aspirations switched from dance to music, and then 'finally she only drew—as if the denied dance came forth from her ever more quietly, ever more discreetly'.[11] In the poems, alongside Orpheus and the narrator of the sonnets, Vera becomes a third image of the driven artist and hence something of a warning to readers not to take the categories and characters of the original myth too rigidly. She is explicitly referred to in sonnets I 25, II 18 and II 28, the last fancifully imagining her ascent into the heavens in death like Orpheus' lyre.

Through the sequence, Rilke identifies the maladies of his early-twentieth-century culture: its alienation from the fact of death and associated emotions such as grief and suffering; its poisonous, still-vital remnants of religious belief; the individual's division from their true self partly through self-consciousness; our divorce from and destruction of Nature and animal life; our over-reliance on technology; the blind eye we too readily turn to injustice and inequality. The diversity of these subjects is what gives this sequence its impressive reach. The poems also devote a great deal of energy to 'praise', a celebration of the visionary joy that this more holistic view of life must yield:

> Be——and know the state of Not-Being too,
> that infinite source of your innermost vibration——
> so you carry it, this once, to completion.
>
> To the used-up——to all Nature's musty and mute,
> its brimming storehouse, its inexpressible sum——
> joyously add yourself and the account's done.

As Charlie Louth has most recently suggested, in reading Rilke 'the poems do not feel aloof [...] They press upon us and make us examine ourselves.'[12] The kind of closed system of a purely aesthetic art, or the kind created by literary 'worship', were this poet's abhorrence. Early in his career, Rilke was already sure that 'art is only a path, it is not a goal'.[13] In a letter of 1903, he likewise confirmed: 'I do not want to tear art and life apart; I know that at any time, in any place, they are one and the same.'[14] Rilke's poetry pays particular attention to the processes of change associated with being human, and his favourite image for such a process is the natural one of 'ripening' or the maturation of wine (especially, in his last years, in poems written in French, the wines of his adopted Valais countryside). His poems record such moments of ripening, but also act, in being read and openly experienced, as opportunities for change to take place in the reading individual. 'What is our job', Rilke once wrote, 'if not, purely and generously, to offer up occasions for change?'[15]

Martyn Crucefix
London, April 2023

Notes

1 S.N. Schill Collection; quoted in *Letters: Summer 1926: Pasternak, Tsvetaeva, Rilke* (NYRB, 2001), pp. 13–14.
2 Marina Tsvetaeva, 'The Poet and His Times', *Volya Rossii* (Paris), 1932; quoted in ibid., p. 21.
3 Letter to Lotte Hepner, 8th November 1915.
4 Letter to Lou, 13th November 1903.
5 Letter to Lou, 8th August 1903.
6 Rilke, *Auguste Rodin* (1903).
7 Ibid.
8 Letter to Witold Hulewicz, 10th November 1925.
9 Ibid.
10 Letter to Countess Margot Sizzo-Noris-Crouy, 12 April 1923.
11 Ibid.
12 Charlie Louth, *Rilke: The Life of the Work* (OUP, 2020), Preface, p. x.
13 Lecture on 'Modern Lyric Poetry', Prague, 1898.
14 Letter to Lou, 11th August 1903.
15 Letter to Thankmar von Münchhausen, 28th June 1915.

FURTHER READING

Rilke's Life

Ralph Freedman, *Life of a Poet: Rainer Maria Rilke* (Northwestern University Press, 1996)

Donald Prater, *A Ringing Glass: The Life of Rainer Maria Rilke* (Clarendon Press, 1986)

Letters of Rainer Maria Rilke: 1892–1910, translated by Jane B. Greene and M.D.H. Norton (Norton, 1969)

Letters of Rainer Maria Rilke: 1910–1926, translated by Jane B. Greene and M.D.H. Norton (Norton, 1969)

Letters: Summer 1926—correspondence associated with Boris Pasternak, Marina Tsvetaeva and Rilke, translated by Margaret Wettlin, Walter Arndt and Jamey Gambrell, preface by Susan Sontag (New York Review of Books, 2001)

Rilke's Works in English Translation

The Book of Hours, translated and introduced by Christine McNeill and Patricia McCarthy (Agenda Editions, 2007)

The Book of Images, translated by Edward Snow (1991; Revised Bilingual Edition, North Point Press, 1994)

The Complete French Poems, translated and introduced by A. Poulin Jr (Graywolf, 1986)

Duino Elegies, translated with a commentary by Martyn Crucefix and introduced by Karen Leeder (Enitharmon Press, 2006)

Duino Elegies, translated by Vita and Edward Sackville-West and introduced by Lesley Chamberlain (1931; Pushkin Press, 2021)

The Essential Rilke, selected and translated by Galway Kinnell and Hannah Liebmann (Ecco Press, 1999)

New Poems, translated by Stephen Cohn and introduced by John Bayley (Carcanet Press, 1992)

New Poems, selected and translated by Edward Snow (1984; 1987; Revised Bilingual Edition, North Point Press, 2001)

The Notebooks of Malte Laurids Brigge, Rilke's semi-autobiographical novel, translated and introduced by Michael Hulse (Penguin Classics, 2009)

Orpheus: A Version of Rilke's Die Sonette an Orpheus, Don Paterson (Faber, 2006)

Poems to Night, edited, translated and introduced by Will Stone (Pushkin Press, 2020)

Selected Poems, translated with an introduction by J.B. Leishman (Penguin Modern European Poets, 1964)

The Selected Poetry of Rainer Maria Rilke, translated by Stephen Mitchell and introduced by Robert Hass (Picador, 1987)

Sonnets to Orpheus, translated with a commentary and introduced by Martyn Crucefix (Enitharmon Press, 2012)

Sonnets to Orpheus with Letters to a Young Poet, translated by Stephen Cohn and introduced by Peter Porter (Carcanet Press, 2000)

Tender Taxes: Versions of Rilke's French Poems, Jo Shapcott (Faber, 2001)

Uncollected Poems, selected and translated by Edward Snow (Bilingual Edition, North Point Press, 1996)

An Unofficial Rilke: Poems 1912–1926, selected, translated and introduced by Michael Hamburger (Anvil Press, 1981)

Critical Books

Chamberlain, Lesley, *Rilke: The Last Inward Man* (Pushkin Press, 2022)

Gass, William, *Reading Rilke: Reflections on the Problems of Translation* (Basic Books, 1999)

Hutchinson, Ben, *Rilke's Poetics of Becoming* (Routledge, 2006)

Leeder, Karen and Vilain, Robert (eds), *The Cambridge Companion to Rilke* (Cambridge University Press, 2010)

Louth, Charlie, *Rilke: The Life of the Work* (OUP, 2020)

TRANSLATOR'S NOTE

This selection of Rilke's poetry has been made with regard to three criteria: those poems a new (or more experienced) reader might reasonably expect to find in such a book, plus those poems that I felt were important to a rich and comprehensive view of Rilke's poetic achievements, plus those individual poems that I felt especially in tune with.

These three criteria were bounded (as they must always be) by the particular translator's competence and confidence in their ability to bring Rilke's German over into English. Given these restraints, I trust this final selection succeeds in including a generous choice of his 'early' poems from 1899 to 1906, through the artistic breakthrough of the *New Poems* (1907/1908), his 'Requiem for a Friend' for Paula Modersohn-Becker (1909), and the not-so-fallow years of 1910 to 1921, a publishing hiatus spectacularly broken in 1922 by the storm of inspiration that completed the *Duino Elegies* and the *Sonnets to Orpheus*. The selection also includes a number of the jewel-like, haiku-like poems Rilke wrote in French in his more settled, brief, final years before his death in 1926.

I do not have much of worth to add here about the process of translation beyond what I said in relation to my 2012 *Sonnets to Orpheus*: there I suggested my goal was to emulate the 'felt shapeliness and musicality' of Rilke's poems with as little sacrifice as possible of their meaning or, more precisely, their semantic and emotional impact. I offered this latest attempt to square the circle of translation to the reader, accompanied only by my approval of Charles Tomlinson's formulation of the task. In introducing his now fifty-year-old translations of Fyodor Tyutchev, he claimed: 'The aim of these translations has been to preserve not the metre, but the movement of each poem—its flight, or track through the mind.'[1]

In broadening the range of my translation task from the 'storm' of 1922 backwards to 1899 and forwards to the mid-1920s, I have been challenged by Rilke's staggering facility with his chosen forms. Early on, I decided that I could not sidestep his use of rhyme as a major component of the work's 'felt shapeliness and musicality'. This has often meant a resort to pararhyme as against the originals' full rhymes. There have also been occasions when the precise sequence of the original rhyming has been replaced with slight variations. But I hope the gain in the impression of (even slightly muffled) Orphic singing outweighs the occasional rejigging.

Notes

1   Charles Tomlinson, *Versions from Fyodor Tyutchev 1803–1873* (OUP, 1960).

FROM
THE BOOK OF MONASTIC LIFE
(1899)

There! The hour inclines and stirs me awake
with its clear, metallic blow:
my senses quivering. I feel: I know—
and I seize the plastic day.

Nothing completed till I beheld it:
all becoming stood still.
My eyes now ripen and, like a bride,
what is wished for will be fulfilled.

I love all things—there is nothing too small,
but boldly I paint it on gold,
and raise it high, and will never know
those in whom it frees the soul...

*

I live my life in ever-widening rings,
encompassing everything, and though I
may not be able to achieve this last thing,
still, I mean to try.

Around God I circle—that age-old, towering form—
a circling thousands of years long;

and still I do not know: am I a hawk, a storm,
or a mighty song.

[...]

You, neighbour God, if I sometimes bother you
in the long night with a sharp knocking,
it's because I often do not hear you breathing
and I know you live alone in that room.
And if you need something, no one is there
to respond to your fumbling, bring you a drink:
I am always listening. Give me the least hint.
I am very near.

There is nothing but a thin wall between us,
and it may be——this might easily happen——
at a cry from your mouth, or one from mine,
that it falls to pieces
without a sound, causing no commotion.

The wall is built from your own images.

And your images are hung round you like names.
And the instant the light flares within me
(in which my depths perceive you more clearly),
it wastes itself, glinting on each picture frame.

And my spirits, fading quickly, growing dim,
are separated from you and have no home.

[...]

You, darkness, out of which I came,
I love you more than the flame
that delineates the world's edge,
with a glimmer
on some sphere,
beyond which no one has more knowledge.

Yet the darkness binds everything into itself:
all forms and flames, creatures and myself,
it seizes upon them,
all powers, all that is human...

And it may be there is an immense might,
stirring nearby—

I believe in the night.

*

I have faith in everything not yet said.
I would set my most devout feelings free.
What none has yet desired, or dared,
will one day come spontaneously to me.

Forgive me, God, if this is presumptuous.
Yet I simply want to tell you this:
my utmost effort will be as an impulse,

33

so without anger or hesitation,
in just the way you are loved by children.

With this spilling forth, this flowing away
into ample arms, into the open sea,
with this surging return,
I will acknowledge you—you, I will proclaim
as none before now has ever done.

And if this is pride, then let me be proud,
but of my prayer—
so solitary and utterly sincere,
in being lifted before your clouded brow.

[…]

Workmen we are—journeyman, pupil, master—
and we build you, you towering nave.
And sometimes, there comes an earnest stranger,
amongst our hundred souls like a lustre,
quivering, and showing us some new way.

We climb up the scaffold's dizzying height,
the hammers in our hands weighing heavy,
until our brows are kissed by a moment,
sent, luminous, as if omniscient,
coming from you like the wind off the sea.

Then the echoing of our many hammers
resounds through the mountains, blow upon blow.
Only with the dark do we let you go:
with the dawning of your emerging contours.

Your greatness, God, we know.

[...]

What will you do, God, when I am gone?
I am your vessel (when I am shattered?)
I am your drink (if I am spilt and scattered?)
I am your business, the clothes you put on,
and in losing me you lose your purpose.

Once I am gone, you will have no house
where words welcome you, intimate and warm,
and the pair of velvet slippers that I am,
loosened, will be lost from your weary feet.

And your coat will no longer button up.
Your glance, that I would always meet
as a warm, consoling pillow for my cheek,
will turn and search, no longer finding me—
and as the sun goes down, there in the lap
of alien stones your bed will be laid.

What will you do, God? I am afraid.

[…]

I know: you are the Inscrutable One,
round whom time stood uncertainly.
Oh, how I made you, so beautifully,
in hours of hard labour for my hand
and pride in my own ability.

I sketched out many a graceful line.
I negotiated every obstacle—
then suddenly my plans turned awry,
grew knotted, thorny as a bramble,
every oval, curve and outline wrong,
till all at once, and deep within me,
from my reaching towards obscurity,
the holiest of all forms sprang.

I cannot review the work I have done,
and my sense is: it is completed.
And yet, with my eyes still averted,
my wish is to begin it all over again.

[…]

Before He creates us, God speaks to each of us just once.
Then, into the night, He goes with us in silence.
Yet these words, at the start,
His cloudy words are:

Propelled by your senses,
go to the very edge of your desire:
bring me clothing.

Behind all things, increase like a fire,
so the shadows they cast are growing:
cover me always.

Let everything happen to you: the beauty and the terror.
Simply keep going: no feeling is too impossibly far.
Do not set a gulf between us.
They call it life, the land
that lies close.

You will know it, and you will understand,
by its seriousness.

Now——give me your hand.

FROM
THE BOOK OF PILGRIMAGE
(1901)

And my soul is a woman in your presence,
is like the cord between Ruth and Naomi.
By day, she tends your harvested sheaves,
labouring like a maid in humble service.
In the evening, she steps down to the river
to bathe, to dress herself, to prepare
to come before you, finding you at peace
and, approaching, she uncovers your feet.
And if you ask her at midnight, she will say,
in deep simplicity: 'I am Ruth, the maid.
Spread your wings above your maid's head.
You are the heir...'

And then my soul sleeps the long night through,
at your feet, where your blood warms her,
and is a woman in your presence—like Ruth.

[...]

And you will inherit the greens
of bygone gardens and the tranquil blues
of dissolving heavens.
And, dropping through a thousand days, the dews,
and the many summers proclaimed by suns,

and the louder springs of sorrow and splendour
as a young girl sets down in her many letters.
You will inherit autumns spread like splendid robes,
in remembrance of poets,
and all winters, like countries long forsaken,
will grow quiet beside you, nestling close.
You will inherit Venice and Rome and Kazan.
Florence will be yours and Pisa's cathedral,
the Lavra Trinity and the Monastir
with its obscure and winding tunnels
far beneath Kyiv's gardens—
and Moscow, with its bells like memories,
and every sound will be yours: the violins,
reeds, horns, every song with the depth to ring
will shine upon you like a precious gem.

And only for you do poets shut themselves in
to gather up images, rich and rustling,
then set out to ripen through comparison,
yet spend their whole lives in seclusion…
And artists only labour at their paintings
so you—who created Nature transient—
might now receive it back, made permanent:
all grows eternal. See, the woman, portrayed
in the Mona Lisa, matured like a wine.
She need never be a woman again—
for no new woman brings anything new.
Those drawn to creation, they are like you.
They wish for eternity. They cry: 'Stone,
be eternal!' And 'Be yours!' is what they mean.

And so too with lovers, they harvest for you:
they are the poets of the passing hour.
They plant a kiss on an expressionless mouth
to make it smile, to create beauty there,
and pleasure too, and they accustom us
to suffering which simply helps us mature.
They bring sorrow beside their laughter,
yearnings that sleep, only to awaken
in another's breast, and it is there they cry.
They gather such mysteries, and then die,
as all creatures do, without comprehending,
yet from them there may spring grandchildren,
within whom their green lives will ripen:
through them, you become heir to the love
they themselves blindly, as if in sleep, gave.

So—the abundance of all things flows to you.
And as with a fountain, the topmost bowl
always over-spills, filling the one below
as if with long and loosened skeins of hair:
abundance, into your valleys, descends to you,
when thoughts and things flood and overflow.

[...]

You are the old man, whose head of hair
is filled with soot, scorched and burnt;
the powerful one, the unremarkable,

43

holding your hammer in your hand.
You are the blacksmith, the song of the year,
standing always ready at the anvil.

You are the one who knows no Sunday,
the one always engaged in labour;
one who might perish because of a blade,
yet unpolished, that must shine brighter.
When the saws stand quiet in the mills
and all the people are drunk and idle,
then the striking of your hammer can still
be heard through town in the peal of bells.

You are the grown-up, you are the master
no one saw practise the mystery;
you are a journeyman, you are a stranger,
about whom gossip and rumours fly,
now boldly, now in no more than a whisper.

[…]

All those who search for you, tempt you.
And those who find you, bind you
with image and gesture.

But simply to apprehend you is all my desire,
as the earth apprehends you;
as I ripen,
your kingdom
ripens too.

I am not asking from you any futile display,
no kind of proof.
I understand time
and you
are not the same.

For my sake, do not perform any kind of miracle.
Lay down the truth of your laws
which—from generation to generation—grows
ever more visible.

[...]

You are the future, the vast red sunrise
above eternity's spreading plain.
After the night of time, you are the cock cry,
the dawn, the dew and the maiden,
the mother and death and the unknown man.

You are the one and ever-shifting figure,
rising above fate, solitary and high,
yet uncelebrated and unmourned for,
and, like a forest wilderness, undescribed.

You are the true epitome of all,
the final word of your being concealed,
and always to each differently revealed:
to the shore as ship and to the ship as landfall.

[...]

The lords of the world are old
and they will leave behind no heir.
Each son dying while still a child,
as their pale-faced daughters offer
sickly crowns to a greater power.
The mob melts them down for money,
the modern world's lord of all,
extruded by fire into machinery,
that, groaning, submits to his will.
Yet happiness eludes them all.
The ore is homesick. It wants to flee
the coins, the cogwheels, the gears
that force it to live in this petty way.
From factories, from cash registers,
it will trace a path back to the veins,
once cut deep into the mountains,
that will fall shut behind it again.

*

All will become great and mighty again:
the landscape easy, the waters will ripple,
the trees stand tall, walls and ramparts small,
and in the valleys—powerful, protean—
a nation of farmers and sheep-herding men.

And churches will no longer clutch at God
like a fugitive, then wail in surprise

to find him a beast, caged and wounded.
Who knocks at the door will be welcomed in
and a spirit of boundless sacrifice
will move you and me and every action.

No more the hereafter and gazing beyond,
only a yearning not to profane death
and to be of service on behalf of the earth,
no longer to feel like strangers in its hand.

[…]

You need not be afraid, God. They say 'mine'
to everything that waits patiently.
They are like the wind brushing through the branches
of a tree and saying, 'all this, my own'.

They fail to see
that everything they take up into their hand
is ablaze, even at its remotest edges,
and they cannot touch it without being burnt.

They say 'mine' in the way one sometimes calls
the prince a friend, talking to a workman,
though the prince is remote and impossibly grand.
They say 'mine' about unfamiliar walls,
though they don't know who owns the houses.
They say 'mine', declaring it all their own,
though, drawing nearer, everything closes.

They are like some ridiculous charlatan,
who declares the sun is his, the lightning too.
Then they announce: here's my dog, my wife,
my child, my life, even though they know
each of these things—dog, wife, child, life—
are unknown objects, into which, at best,
they have blundered, blindly, hands outstretched.
Only the wise truly realize these things,
with their longing to see. And as for the rest,
they don't want to be told their poor wanderings
are not really connected to anything,
and that—cast off by every possession,
forever unacknowledged by their own—
they cannot 'have' a woman or the rose's bloom,
whose life, in truth, to us all is alien.

So, God, do not lose your equilibrium.
Even one who glimpses your face in darkness,
one who loves you, yet, like a candle flame,
staggers before your breath, cannot possess you.
And if another, at night, is reaching for you,
trying to compel you to enter his prayer:
                    you are the guest,
                    you can shift elsewhere.

Who can hold you, God? For you are your own
and, from the least touch of ownership, quite free,
like a wine, as it matures, belonging
to nothing but itself as it grows more sweet.

FROM
THE BOOK OF POVERTY AND DEATH
(1903)

So it is, Lord, that our major cities are
all laid to waste and lost to dissipation:
the greatest of them is like fleeing a fire,
for there is no consolation, no care,
and their petty season is winding down.

There, men live in wretched basement rooms,
brutal lives, full of fearful gestures,
more apprehensive than first-born lambs;
while outside, your earth breathes and observes,
yet they must go on living, unawares.

There, children grow up, beyond windows,
forever darkened by the self-same shadows,
(not knowing that, outside, flowers call them
to freedom, days of joy, where the wind blows):
yet children they must be, mournful children.

There, young girls bloom into the unknown,
wishing for the quiet of their childhood;
yet what they burn for cannot be found
and so, trembling, they close back up again.
In shrouded back rooms, they must live out
their days of disenchanted motherhood,

51

the endless nights of weeping helplessness,
the bleak years without the strength to fight.
And off in the gloom, their deathbeds await,
and eventually they come to crave them,
and they pass slowly, dying as if in chains,
their vanishing like that of a beggar woman.

*

There, people live, pale-faced, petal-white,
and dying in awe of the world's weight.
And no one notices the gaping grimace
into which the smiles of a gentle race
are twisted with each anonymous night.

They roam to and fro, degraded by labours.
They serve futile things without courage,
their clothes hanging limply from their shoulders,
and their lovely hands prematurely aged.

The crowd rushes on, never stopping to help,
though they appear so fearful and frail.
Only shy dogs, belonging nowhere else,
trail behind them silently for a while.

By a hundred things, they are tormented
and abused at the stroke of every bell.
In dread of the day they will be admitted,
they hurry alone past the hospital.

Death is there. But not one they once met,
miraculously, were touched by, as children:
only petty death, as they there conceive it.
Their real death hangs, not yet sweet, still green
like a fruit within that will not ripen.

[...]

Yet the cities crave only what is their own,
and in their wake they pull everything down.
They smash creatures like rotten timbers,
and consume whole nations in their fires.

And their populations serve their wishes,
losing all sense of harmony and balance,
finding progress in their own snail traces,
driving faster where they walked slowly once,
feeling like whores, tricked out in cheap dresses,
racketing louder amongst steel and glass.

Each day—as if duped by some delusion—
they no longer behave like themselves.
Money, stealing all their strength, increases
like a powerful east wind, and with time,
hollowed, weakened, they await the wine,
all the poison of human and bestial juices,
to goad them back to their fleeting business.

[...]

Oh, where is he, the one whose power rose,
beyond time and possessions, in being poor,
who shed his clothes in the market square,
and stood naked before the bishop's robes.
Most loving of all men, and most tender,
coming to live with us like the young year.
The brown-clad brother of your nightingale,
in whom there grew delight and rapture,
who found his joy on earth, in this world.

For he was never one of the ever weary:
with each passing day they grow more joyless.
Amongst flowers, as with little brothers,
along the meadow's edge, he made his way,
and spoke of himself, how he would apply
himself, in hope of bringing joy to all.
There was no end to his luminous soul,
and nothing was too small to be passed by.

He came from light to more profound light,
and cheerfulness flooded his narrow cell.
And upon his face, ever broader, a smile
that betrayed his history, from childhood,
as if maturing, towards maidenhood.

And when he sang, what had been forgotten,
even yesterday, returned once again,

and on the nests of birds fell such stillness,
a crying out only in the hearts of holy sisters
whom he'd touched as might a bridegroom.

And from his red mouth, then, was let loose
the pollen of his song, softly released,
dreamingly, drifting to those loving ones,
falling into their gaping corollas,
slowly sinking to the depths of their blooms.

And they received him, this unblemished one,
each into their flesh, as into their souls.
And their eyes closed like the petals of roses,
and their hair was filled with nights of love.

And all things, great and small, welcomed him.
To many creatures there came cherubim,
in the guise of beautiful butterflies,
proclaiming their females would bear young:
by all these creatures he was recognized,
and they each had their fruitfulness from him.

And in death, plainly, as if namelessly,
he was dispersed: his seed went gushing down
into the streams and sang from every tree
and gazed quietly at him from every bloom.
He lay, singing. And the sisters stood round
and wept for him, their beloved husband.

FROM
THE BOOK OF IMAGES
(1902; 1906)

Entrance

Whoever you are: in the evening, step out
of your living room and all that's familiar;
yours, the last house before the truly remote:
no matter who you are.
And though your eyes have grown so weary,
hard to raise them from the worn threshold,
slowly, with them, you lift up a black tree
and set it before the sky: lean and alone.
And you have made a world. And it is immense,
like a word, in silence, that continues to grow.
And as your will grasps its significance,
so your eyes, tenderly, let it go...

The Guardian Angel

You are the bird whose broad wings came
when I called at night, stirred from sleep,
calling only with my arms, for your name
is like an abyss, a thousand nights deep.
You are the shade I sleep in, hushed and calm,
your seed woven through my every dream:
you are the image, but I am the frame
that completes you in glittering relief.

What do I call you? See, my lips are numb.
You are the origin that floods and pours,
while I am the slow, apprehensive 'amen'
that timidly rounds out your splendours.

Often you roused me from my sombre rest,
when sleep felt more like a grave to me,
like taking flight, or becoming lost;
you raised me then from the obscurities
of the heart, wished to hoist me to the top
of all towers like a scarlet flag in the breeze.

You speak of wonders as of certainties,
and of people as if they were melodies,
and of roses: of things

taking place in the blazing of your gaze.
You, blessed one, when will you summon Him,
the remnants of whose glories,
from the seventh and the last of His days,
like a radiance can still be descried
in the beating of your wings…

Or is your command that I call Him?

The Saint

The people parched. The only young woman
without thirst, set out amongst the stones,
imploring water for the whole nation.
But the willow branch she held made no signs,
and exhausted now, by how far she'd come,
at last, she thought only of one suffering
(a sick boy and, as if by premonition,
they had gazed at each other one evening).
In that instant, the willow sapling bucked
in her hands like a thirsting creature:
now she walked on, blooming above her blood,
with her blood roaring deeply within her.

From a Childhood

The darkness grew like riches in the room
where, perfectly hidden, the boy was sat.
And as the mother entered, as in a dream,
a glass trembled in the silent cabinet.
She was aware that the room betrayed her,
and she bent to kiss her boy: Are you here?
Then both glanced at the piano in fear,
for many an evening the song she played
would strangely, deeply, captivate the child.

He sat very still. His widening gaze
hung on her hand which, with its ring, bent low,
and, as if labouring through drifts of snow,
travelled across the white keys.

The Last Supper

Astonished, perturbed, they have assembled
round him and like a sage he has chosen
to withdraw from those to whom he once belonged,
and now will pass strangely beyond them.
For him, the old sensation of being alone,
the feeling that inspired his profound deed;
now he'll walk again through the olive grove
and, before him, those who love him will flee.

He has summoned them to this last meal
and (as a gunshot scares birds from a cornfield)
he scatters their reaching hands from the bread
with his word: they fly towards him, afraid,
they flutter to and fro round the table
for some way out. But like the twilight hour,
the truth is *he* is everywhere.

People at Night

The nights are not made for the crowd.
You are divided from your neighbour by the night,
and ought not to seek him out.
And after dark, if you flood your house with light,
to see human faces in a clearer view,
first you should consider: who?

People are dreadfully disfigured by the light,
dripping from their faces,
and when they are gathered together at night,
all you see in such places
is a tottering world, simply flung together.
And across their brows, a yellow glimmer
has displaced all thought,
and in every glance, the flickering of wine,
and their hands, fraught,
are weighed down by gestures with which they try
to understand each other
in the course of conversation,
in which they say: *I* and *I*
and mean anyone.

Pont du Carrousel

The blind man who is standing on the bridge,
grey as a milestone from some nameless land,
is the thing, perhaps, forever unchanging,
that the starry hours spin remotely around,
the clear focal point of the constellations.
Round him everything flits and gleams and runs.

He is the sole upright, the thing unmoved,
set down amongst so many confounding ways:
the obscure entrance to the underworld
in the midst of a superficial race.

Autumn Day

Lord: it is time. The summer was very long.
Lay your shadows across the sundials,
and let the winds blow free across the fields.

Instruct the last of the fruits to ripen:
give them two more days of this southerly clime,
and urge them on towards perfection,
chase the last sweetness into the heavy wine.

No time now to build for those left homeless.
Who remains alone now will find no relief,
but will watch and read and write long letters,
and roam here and there on the windswept streets,
restlessly, while the leaves are cast adrift.

On the Edge of Night

My room and these expanses
of night's estate, awakening,
are one. I am a string,
stretched and sounding,
over whispering resonances.

Things are violin-bodies
filled with a darkness, murmuring:
within it, dreaming, the weeping of women;
within it, roused from sleep,
the rancour of whole dynasties...
I tremble
like silver: then all
will shiver beneath me,
and whatever has lost its way
in things will aspire towards the light
which, from my dancing tone,
around which the heavens pulse,
down through narrow and aching vents,
into the ancient
abysses,
endlessly falls...

Prayer

Night, quiet night, into which are woven
all white things, red things, things brightly hued,
scattered colours, and each and every one
raised to One Darkness, One Stillness—include
me also and weave me into a relation
with the many you entice and secure.
Do my senses still play with light too often?
If they do, then must my face forever
stand out, disturbing, amongst the elements?
By my hands, I would prefer you to judge me:
do they not lie there like instruments,
like things? And is the ring not plain to see
upon my hand, and does the light cast on them
not lie precisely so, and full of trust,
as if they were paths, and as if they gleamed,
and took no other turn but into darkness? ...

Evening in Skåne

The park is high. And, as if leaving a room,
I walk, emerging from its twilit gloom
to open ground and evening. Into the wind,
the same the clouds must feel in passing by,
and to gleaming rivers and mills that grind
slowly, spinning at the edge of the sky.
Now I too am a thing held in its hand,
the minutest of all things—yet look here:

is this one heaven?
                 Blissfully blue and clear,
into which purer and purer clouds rise,
white colours shifting along their undersides,
while up above vast and airy greys run
to flow warmly as across a red primer,
and over it all the declining sun,
casting its calm radiance.

                 Miraculous
structure: shifting within itself, it sustains
itself, builds vast figures, and mountains,
and wings furled before the first stars show,
and now: a door into such remoteness,
as perhaps only the birds know…

Evening

The evening is slowly changing its clothes,
held for it by a rim of ancient trees;
you watch: and the earth, growing distant, moves,
this slipping from you, this lifted to the skies;

and leaves you, a part of nothing wholly,
not so dark as the house in its silence,
not so surely invoking eternity
as that which becomes star each night and rises;

and leaves you (beyond words to unravel),
your life, immense, ripening, full of fear,
so that, now bounded and now embracing all,
it becomes in you alternately stone and star.

Annunciation

the words of the angel

You are no closer to God than we;
we all stand at a distance.
And yet, how wonderfully
are your hands blessed.
No woman's ripen in this way,
radiantly from the sleeve:
I am the dew, I am the day,
but you, you are the tree.

I am weary, my way was long;
forgive me, I've forgotten
what He, arrayed in gold,
enthroned like the sun,
wanted me to say, pensive one
(as if this room confused me).
See: I am the beginning,
but you, you are the tree.

I stretched out my wings,
wider than I'd ever known;
now your tiny house brims
with my ample robes.
And yet, you are more alone
than ever, hardly see me;

then: I am a breath in a grove,
but you, you are the tree.

The angels, trembling in fear,
let go of each other:
never longing such as this,
so vast, so precarious.
Perhaps something will happen
you grasp only in dream.
Hail to you, my soul perceives:
you are readied, prepared,
like a gateway, tall and wide,
and soon you will fall open.
You, my song's sweetest ear,
I feel now: my word, lost
in you, deep, as in a forest.

So, I came and accomplished
your thousand and one dreams.
God looked on me: He dazzled...

But you, you are the tree.

Those of the House of Colonna

You, strangers, men who now stand motionless
in pictures, you once cut such a fine figure
on horseback, strode impatiently through the house;
like a handsome dog, with that same air,
your hands hanging beside you now, in repose.

Your faces seem so charged with watching,
because the world was image upon image for you;
from flags and fruit, weaponry and women,
this great confidence sprang up in you:
that all things *are* and that all things *are true*.

Yet back then, in days when you were too young
to take part in important battles,
and too young to wear the papal purple,
not always lucky in hunting or riding,
boys still, who denied themselves to women—
of those boyish times,
nothing? Not one single recollection?

Do you not remember how it was back then?

In those days there was the altar
in a secluded aisle,

Mary giving birth in the picture.
And you, beguiled
by the tendrils of a bloom,
and by the thought
that, in solitude, the fountain,
under the light of the moon,
flinging up its waters in the garden,
was like a world.

The window swung open at your feet like a door.
And all was parkland, with paths and meadows
off in the distance, and yet strangely close,
and strangely luminous, and yet as if obscure,
and the fountains murmuring like the rain,
and it was as if morning would never come again
to bring an end to the long night,
where it stood beneath all the stars' glimmering light.

Flourishing in those days, boys, how your hands
grew warm. (Though you did not know it.)
In those days, your faces stood wide open.

FROM
NEW POEMS I
(1907)

To Karl and Elisabeth Von der Heydt in friendship

Early Apollo

As may often happen, a morning peers
through still-leafless branches and already
there is spring: so, for now, nothing obscures,
in his head, the lustre of all poetry,

its impact upon us, so nearly fatal;
for there is as yet no shadow in his gaze,
his temples for now too cool for laurel,
and it will be some while before the rose

garden will grow up tall above that brow,
before one leaf, then another detaches,
drifting down towards the trembling mouth,

which is as yet still unused and flashes
only with his smile's drinking something in,
as if his song were being instilled in him.

The Departure of the Prodigal Son

Now, to leave behind all this confusion,
that is ours and yet never belonged to us,
that like the waters of an ancient fountain
reflect us, then, trembling, the image blurs;
from all this, as if entangled in thorns
that catch at us, over and over, to turn
away from it all,
from this and this,
and from all these things you hardly notice
(all so commonplace, merely everyday),
now seeming tender and conciliatory,
as if grown closer, as at some beginning,
and to see, in truth, it was not personal,
how everyone experienced suffering,
even childhood filled with it to the brim.
And still to turn, hand from hand, to go,
as if freshly tearing something just healed,
to depart: to where? Into the unknown,
to some strange, far-off, temperate land
that beyond all action will simply stand
as indifferent backdrop: a wall, a garden;
to leave: why? from impulse, from nature,
from dark anticipation, impatience,
incomprehension, even out of ignorance?

To take all this upon yourself, and it may be
in vain, letting slip what you have, to die,
perhaps, all alone, still not knowing why:

Is this really the way to a new life?

Pieta

So, Jesus, I look upon your feet again,
which before were the feet of a young man,
when I nervously stripped and bathed them;
how they became entangled in my hair
and were like two white deer in a briar.

So I look on your never-beloved limbs,
on this night of love, for the first time.
We never, before now, lay together,
and now it is only to gaze and admire.

But see, your hands are torn, beloved,
though not from any love-bite of mine.
Your heart lies open, any may be admitted:
that should have been my way in alone.

Now you are weary and your tired mouth
has no desire for my mouth with its cry:
Oh, Jesus, my Jesus, when was our hour?
Each brought to ruin in this wondrous way.

Buddha

As if he were listening. Silence: far off…
We stop and we no longer hear anything.
And he is star. And standing all round him,
other great stars we can see nothing of.

Oh, he is all things. Really, do we loiter
in hope he sees us? Would he feel the need?
If we threw ourselves down before him here,
he would remain unmoved, still as a beast.

For what drives us to gather at his feet
has spun through him for millions of years.
All we know is something he once forgot,
and all he knows of wisdom is not ours.

God in the Middle Ages

And within themselves they kept him safe,
and wanted him to be, to determine,
and they hung him eventually with weights
(intending to prevent his ascension),

with the burden of their vast cathedrals.
So encumbered, all they required of him
was to revolve above boundless creation
like a clock, to give signs and signals,

to help with their concerns, their day's work.
But suddenly, roused into life, he burst
upon the people of the stricken city

who, terrified by his voice, set him free,
leaving the clockwork to become disengaged,
and fled from what they read in his face.

The Panther

in the Jardin des Plantes, Paris

With pacing the bars back and forth, his gaze
grows so tired there is nothing it can hold.
To him, there appear to be a thousand bars,
and beyond the thousand bars, no world.

The lithe, smooth steps of his powerful gait
that, within the smallest of circles, spins round,
is like a dance of power about a point
at which an immense will stands, stunned.

Only in moments does the pupil's curtain
slide noiselessly open—then an image enters,
passing through the tense silence of each limb
into the heart, where it disappears.

The Gazelle

Gazella Dorcas

Enchanted one: how could the harmony
of two chosen words ever match the rhyme
that comes and goes within you? The way
branch and lyre start from your brow like a sign

and every part of you is like a lover's song,
the words falling tenderly as the rose
lets drop petals on one who does not read on,
but, shutting his eyes, lets the book close

to gaze at you: as if each shapely leg
were a shotgun, loaded with leap after leap,
undischarged, while your head tilts on your neck,

listening, alert: a girl who has ventured deep
into a wood, startled by sounds as she bathes,
the glint of forest pool on her upturned face.

Saint Sebastian

Like a figure reclining, he stands there,
held entirely by his absolute faith.
With the far-off look of a nursing mother,
and yet wrapped in himself like a wreath.

And the arrows fly: now and now again,
so many, as if sprouting from his thighs,
iron heads quivering to their free ends.
Even so, unscathed, he darkly smiles.

Only once does any grief begin to show:
his eyes widen in the face of this suffering,
till they repudiate this pitiful thing,
and as if scornfully they let them go,
those who would destroy a beautiful thing.

Roman Sarcophagi

And yet what is it that stops us believing
(set down here as we are, so disposed)
that anger and hatred and confusion
linger only for a short while within us,

as once, in this ornate sarcophagus,
with its slow-mouldering robes and ribbons,
its glassware and rings and divine images,
something lay in slow dissolution—

until swallowed up by the unknown mouths
that never speak. (Where does the mind exist
that one day will conceive a use for them?)

Then the eternal water was released
in them from the old aqueducts so that now
it runs and dazzles and glints in each one.

The Swan

This labouring through tasks not yet complete,
ponderously, and as if constrained,
resembles the swan's awkward walking gait.

And so, dying, this no longer holding on
to the earth upon which we stand every day,
his timorous settling of himself down:

into the waters that receive him gently
and, as if they passed away, happily,
retreating beneath him like a rippling tide;
while he, infinitely calmly and assured,
ever more majestically and more mature,
is content, the more serenely, to glide.

Going Blind

She sat there with the others, taking tea.
And beside the others, it seemed, at first,
that she held out her cup differently.
At one point she smiled. It almost hurt.

And when at last they rose from their chairs,
slowly, still talking, as it so happened,
(laughing and chattering) to rooms elsewhere,
I noticed her again. How she trailed behind,

reticent, more like a woman compelled
to sing before a great crowd of people.
On her clear, delighted eyes the light fell
from outside as if reflected in a pool.

She followed on, slowly, taking her time,
as if something further had to be overcome,
and yet: as if, after that transition,
she would no longer have to walk but fly.

Experience of Death

We understand nothing of this departure
that gives nothing away. We have no grounds
for showing love, or hatred, or wonder,
in the face of death, so curiously changed

by the tragic masks to grim lamentation.
Still, the world is full of roles we take on.
All the while we strive for approbation,
Death plays too, although he pleases no one.

And yet, when you departed this scene,
a shaft of reality burst through the rift
you created by leaving: green, real green,
a real forest, with real sunshine, brightly lit.

We go on acting. We anxiously proclaim
our hard-learnt roles, the occasional gesture,
yet, remotely, and with no part in our play,
there are times we sense your presence here,

coming upon us like an acknowledgement
of the reality that settles around us,
so that, enraptured, for a brief moment,
we play to the life, no thought of applause.

Blue Hydrangea

Like the last dregs in a pot of green paint,
these leaves are shabby, dry and lacklustre,
behind the heads of flowers that display
no blue, but merely reflect it from afar.

They reflect it imperfectly, tear-stained,
as if they wanted to lose it again,
and, just as with old, blue stationery,
there are touches of yellow, violet and grey;

like the colours in a child's pinafore dress,
now past its best, never to be worn again:
so we feel life's brevity for the young.

And yet, suddenly, the blue seems reborn
in one of the flower heads and you glimpse
a touching blue, delighting before the green.

Buddha

The shy, foreign pilgrim, from a distance,
already senses gold dripping from him;
as if—filled with remorse for their sins—
vast empires had heaped up their riches.

Yet more astonished, the closer he gets,
standing before the brows' magnificence:
for there is no trace here, no evidence,
of wives' gold earrings or drinking goblets.

Is there any who would know what things were
collected, and then melted down, to create
this image in its flower-shaped chalice:

more softly yellow, more inclined to silence,
than any golden object, and everywhere
communing, as with itself, with this space.

Roman Fountain

Borghese

Two basins, one placed above the other,
within a curved rim of ancient marble,
and the water, softly, from the higher
spilling down to the waiting water below,

responding mutely to the soft-spoken one
and, as it were, in the cup of its hand,
showing him, secretly, the sky beyond,
the green, the shadow, like something unknown;

quietly spreading in its splendid bowl,
circle on circle, without longing for home,
only trickling sometimes as in a dream

to let itself down over the mossy rim
into the final mirror and, with its passing,
drawing from the pool below a gentle smile.

The Carousel

Jardin du Luxembourg

Under the shadows cast by its canopy,
the band of bright-coloured horses runs round
for a while, each of them from that country
that lingers a long time before sinking down.
Of course, some are hitched to wagons behind,
yet all show courage in their expression:
a fierce red lion is running alongside them,
and a white elephant now, there and gone.

There is even a deer, as if in a wood,
though he wears a saddle upon his back,
on which a little blue girl has been strapped.

And riding the lion, a boy in white,
who holds on tight with his hot little hand:
the lion showing its teeth, tongue hanging out.

And a white elephant now, there and gone.

And on several horses that go speeding by
are bright girls too, though they have already
almost outgrown these prancing steeds and ride
while gazing off, somewhere else, far away—

And a white elephant now, there and gone.

And so it continues, hurrying to be done,
whirling and spinning with no destination.
A red horse passes, a green, then a grey,
there, a small face in profile, hardly begun,
and a smile, occasionally, turning this way,
such a blissful one, dazzling, gone to waste
on this blind, utterly breathtaking game...

Spanish Dancer

Like a match being struck in a cupped hand
flares white at first before the flame's shivering
tongue darts, penetrates—starting to dance
within the close-packed round of the audience,
she spins, suddenly bright, hot, flickering.

And instantly the room is filled with flame.

With just a glance, she sets her hair ablaze
with daring artistry, suddenly she makes
her whole dress burst into a swirl of flame,
out of which—like startled serpents—arise
her naked arms, thrusting and rattling.

And then: as if the blaze has reached its height,
she brings it together and flings it down,
with such an imperious gesture of pride,
and glares: there it lies, raging on the ground,
and still alight, yet refusing to die:
in assured triumph, with what seems a sweet
smile of salute, she tosses her head high,
and stamps it out under her small, hard feet.

Tombs of the Hetaerae

In long swathes of their own hair they lie,
with earthen-brown, deep, withdrawn faces.
Eyes closed as if from too much distance.
Skeletons, mouths, flowers. In their mouths,
the straight teeth arranged in tidy rows
like ivory figures in a travelling chess set.
And flowers, yellow pearls, slender bones,
hands and tunics, the decaying fabrics
over the caved-in heart. But beneath rings,
talismans, eye-blue stones (precious keepsakes),
the silent crypt of the sex still stands,
filled to its domed roof with flower petals.
Yellow pearls again, unstrung, scattered,
bowls of fired clay round the rims of which
were painted their own images, green shards
of perfume jars with the smell of flowers,
and statues of tiny gods: household altars,
the hetaerae heavens of ravished gods.
Torn-open girdles lie beside flat scarabs,
little figures sporting huge phalluses,
a laughing mouth, athletes and dancers,
golden brooches that resemble tiny bows
for hunting bird- and beast-shaped amulets,
long pins, decorative household implements,
the ruddy ground of a rounded potsherd

on which run—like the black inscription
above a door—the stiff legs of a four-in-hand.
And again flowers, more scattered pearls,
the gleaming, curved limbs of a small lyre,
and, between the veils, settling like mists,
as if just emerged from the shoe's chrysalis,
an ankle joint like a fragile butterfly.

And so they lie, full to the brim with things,
jewels, valuables, toys, household goods,
broken trinkets (all that slipped into them),
each having grown dark as a riverbed.

And riverbeds they were—
above them, in short-lived, impetuous waves
(each wanting to survive to the next life),
the bodies of many young men tumbled,
and streams of grown men surged through them.
And boys, sometimes, escaping the mountains
of childhood, descended, in timid streams,
to play with what they found on the riverbed,
until its long incline was all they knew:

then they filled with smooth and limpid water
across the whole width of this ample way,
eddies spinning through their deepest reaches,
and, for the first time, reflecting the banks
and cries of far-off birds while, high above,
night after starry night of a sweet land
flourished in skies that nowhere reached an end.

Orpheus. Eurydice. Hermes.

This was the extraordinary mine of souls.
Resembling silent, silver ores, they spread
like veins through its darkness. Between the roots
sprang the blood that makes its way towards men,
seeming heavy as porphyry in the gloom.
Nothing else was red.

There were cliffs
and incorporeal forests. There were bridges
over nothing and that vast, grey, blind lake
that hung, suspended over its remote bed
like a rain-filled sky above a landscape.
And between meadows, soft, and full of patience,
the pale line of a single path appeared
like a bleached, long-winding ribbon.

And this was the path they moved along.

In front, the slender man in the blue cloak,
who silently, impatiently looked ahead.
His stride consumed the way in great chunks
without stopping to chew; his hands hung,
heavy and clenched beyond the falling folds,
no longer conscious of the delicate lyre

that had grown to become one with his left
as roses twine through the boughs of an olive.
And his senses were as if divided:
while sight ran on before him like a dog,
to spin round, come back, then speed off again,
only to stand, waiting, at the next turn,
his hearing lagged behind him like a scent.
In moments, it seemed to him it reached
back to the footsteps of the other two,
who were to follow him the whole way up.
Or was it just the echo of his own climbing,
his cloak flapping behind him in the breeze.
He told himself they were still coming;
he spoke aloud, hearing himself die away.
They must be there, though they both moved
so dreadfully quietly. If he could just
once turn back (though one backward look
would utterly destroy the entire work
now being accomplished), he must see them,
the two quiet ones, silently following:

the god of ways and of far-flung messages,
the traveller's cap down over his bright eyes,
the slender staff held out before him,
and the beating of wings around his ankles;
and there, entrusted to his left hand, *her*.

The so-beloved that, from a single lyre,
more grief rose up than from mourning women;

of that grief a whole world was created,
in which all lived once more: wood and valley,
village and highway, field and beast and stream;
and far round this lamentation-world,
there revolved, as around the other earth,
a sun and a silent, star-filled heaven,
a lament-heaven with its own marred stars—
this so-beloved.

But now she walked at the god's left hand,
her steps constrained by her trailing shroud,
softly, uncertain, and without impatience.
She was deep in herself, as with a great hope,
with no thought of the man who walked ahead,
nor of the path that climbed up towards life.
She was in herself. And her being dead
fulfilled her, as it were, with abundance.
Like a fruit with its sweetness and darkness,
she was filled with the greatness of her death,
so new to her she understood nothing.

She had come into a new virginity,
and was untouchable; her sex had closed
like a young flower at the approach of night,
and her hands had grown so unaccustomed
to marriage that even the gentle god's
infinitely tender and guiding touch
pained her, such intimacy was too much.

She was already no longer the fair woman,
who sometimes sounded in the poet's songs,
no longer the wide bed's scent and island,
and no longer was she that man's possession.

Already, she was spilt loose as long hair,
poured out in abandon like falling rain,
and bestowed as a limitless supply.

She was already root.

And when—abruptly—
the god halted her and, with a pained cry,
he uttered the words: 'He has turned around',
she could not understand and said softly: *Who?*

Yet, off in the distance, a dark shape stood
at the bright exit, someone whose features
were unrecognizable. He stood, watching,
as on the narrow ribbon of the meadow path,
with a grieving look, the messenger god
turned silently to follow the figure
already walking back the way she had come,
her steps constrained by her trailing shroud,
softly, uncertain, and without impatience.

The Bowl of Roses

You have seen anger flare, seen the figures
of two boys, bundling themselves to a thing
of hatred, writhing together on the floor
like a beast set upon by a swarm of bees:
performers, heaped-up, exaggerators,
furious horses, crashed upon the ground,
eyes rolling, teeth bared, as if the skull
would peel itself out of the gaping mouth.

But now you know how to forget such things:
for before you stands the bowl of roses,
which is unforgettable and suffused
with that utmost of being, and bending,
of yielding, and withholding, of being here,
that may perhaps be ours: our utmost too.

A soundless life that arises without rest
to inhabit space, without stealing space
from the space that other things diminish,
all but lacking outline, as if omitted,
full of pure inwardness, strange, delicate,
and to its very edge apparent to itself:
do we know anything resembling this?

And then like this: a sensation that rises
from the mere touch of petal on petal?
And this: where one opens like an eyelid
and, lying beneath, all the other eyelids
tightly shut, as if such tenfold slumber
might subdue some bright inward vision.
And this, above all: that through these petals
light must pass. From a thousand heavens,
slowly they screen every speck of darkness
in whose fiery glow the tangled bundles
of stamens rouse themselves and grow erect.

And look, such animation in the roses:
gestures, with such angles of deflection
they would pass unnoticed, but for the fact
their rays are diffused through the universe.

Look at that white one, opened joyously,
and standing with its great, spreading petals
like a Venus upright in her curved shell;
and this one, blushing, as if perplexed,
tilts its head towards this cooler-hued one,
and how aloofly the cool one withdraws,
and how this cold one stands, wrapped in itself,
amongst opened ones that shed everything.
And *what* they shed, how it may be light,
or heavy, it may be a cloak, or burden,
a wing, or a mask, it depends, and *how* they
do this: as if standing before a lover.

What can they not be? Was that yellow one,
lying there, cupped like a bowl, not the skin
of some fruit of which the same yellow
was the juice, concentrated to orange-red?
And was that one's opening into the air
too much already, so that its nameless pink
took on the sour aftertaste of lilac?
And that cambric one, is it not a dress
beneath which the shift is still warm and soft
as the breath with which it was slipped off
in the morning shade by the old forest pool?
And that opalescent, porcelain one,
as fragile as a dainty china cup,
and brimming with tiny, bright butterflies,
and that, containing nothing but itself?

Are they not all alike: containing nothing
but themselves, if to contain themselves means
to transform the outer world, wind and rain,
and patience of spring, guilt, restlessness,
the veiled fate, darkening evening of the earth,
to the shift and flight and approach of clouds,
to the dim influence of distant stars,
all this into a handful of inwardness?

Laid carefree now amongst the open roses.

FROM
NEW POEMS II: THE OTHER PART
(1908)

To my great friend Auguste Rodin

Archaic Torso of Apollo

We did not know his extraordinary head,
in which the eyeballs once ripened. And yet,
his torso is like a candelabra, ablaze,
preserving, hardly diminished, his gaze,

glowing still. Otherwise, the breast's curved prow
could not dazzle you and, from the slight turn
of his hips, a smile could not be let go
to that centre, the site of procreation.

Otherwise, stone would stand shorn, defaced,
beneath the sheer incline of each shoulder,
and would not glisten like a predator's fur,

and would not burst its bounds on every side
like a star: because there is no place
that does not see you. You must change your life.

Leda

As the god entered it in his distress,
he was all but shocked by the swan's beauty;
still, he let himself vanish, perplexed.
Deceit already impelled him to the deed,

even before he could explore the feeling
of this untried life. And the vulnerable one,
she saw already who came to her in the swan
and knew already: he desired one thing

which she, in her resistance, confounded,
could no longer keep from him. Down he swept,
necking past her hand, growing ever weaker,

until the god spent himself in the beloved.
Only then did he find delight in his feathers,
only then became true swan in her lap.

Dolphins

Those realists were happy for their kind
to thrive, content that they lived anywhere,
sharing a sense of kinship, they found signs
of their peers in the ocean's fluid empire,
which the old sea god, with dripping tritons,
would sometimes stir to tempest and flood;
for there surfaced the creature that showed
itself to be far more than the dumb,
dull-witted breed of fish: blood of their blood,
and distantly inclined to the human.

A school of them, rolling, leaping, appeared,
seeming conscious of the glittering sea:
joyful, trusting, warm-blooded, they wreathed
the sea voyage with their brave assembly
and would sport round the ship's prow with ease,
as if tracing the curved outlines of a vase,
heedless, blessed, never fearing injury,
now enraptured, breaching, speeding along
and diving deep as if to exchange places
with the waves that calmly bore the trireme on.

And the sailors took these newly discovered
friends into their lives of lonely hazard

and they contrived for these companions—
and believed it true—a world of gratitude,
in which they loved gods and music and gardens
and the year's silent, deep constellations.

The Death of the Beloved

About death he knew just what we all know:
that it takes us and thrusts us into silence.
But when she was not snatched from him so
violently, no, softly slipped from his eyes,

drifting into the shadows of the unknown,
and when he felt they had her safely there,
still possessed of her kindly manner
and that girlish smile of hers, bright as a moon,

then the dead became familiar to him
as if, through her, somehow, he had become kin
to them all. He would let others exclaim,

yet would not believe, and that realm he named
the well situated, the ever sweet,
and he would search there for a trace of her feet.

The Reliquary

Outside, a keen waiting for all the rings,
an eagerness for each link in the chain,
for destiny does not unfold without them.
Inside, there are objects, nothing but things,
even the crown, set up before the smith,
is something he has had to work and craft,
an object merely, though a trembling one,
to be raised with a scowl, as if in wrath,
to stand as a foil to some perfect stone.

His eyes have grown cold and colder still
from the chill of what he drank day and night;
yet the moment the splendid receptacle
(of the purest gold, embossed, exquisite)
stood finished before him, a votive gift,
designed to house the miraculous, white,
minuscule bone from a dead man's wrist,

he found he could not get up off his knees,
prostrate, afraid to do more than weep,
to bow and scrape, he cast his soul down
before the serenity of the ruby
that seemed to watch him, even to question
his existence, regarding him suddenly
as if with the gaze of remote dynasties.

Crucifixion

Long used to corralling the local scum
up the barren slope of the gallows' hill,
the brawny henchmen stood round for a while,
only a blank face turning now and then

to where the three were to be executed.
Up there, the grisly hanging business
was quickly over; still, the men loitered,
with nothing more to do, they were at a loss.

Then one (as if draped in a butcher's apron,
blood-spattered) shouted: 'Hey, Cap, this one called!'
High on his horse, 'Which one?' asked the captain,
and yet it was as if he too had heard

him crying out: Elijah! Then everybody
jumped up and came crowding round to see
the end, though fearful of too quick a death,
pouring all the vinegar-gall in his mouth,
even as he struggled for his last breath:

because they hoped for a full performance,
perhaps even the coming of Elijah.
Beyond them, Mary screamed in the distance,
and he, himself, roared once and expired.

In the Asylum Garden

Dijon

The walls of the abandoned monastery
still enclose the courtyard, something intact.
For those who now live there, still a retreat,
a place turned away from the life beyond it.

Whatever may have happened, come and gone.
They walk familiar paths now, pleased
to bid goodbye, then greet each other again,
as if circling, simply, quite happily.

Though some tend to the beds of spring flowers,
gently, humbly, going down on their knees,
yet they perform—as long as no one sees—
curious, secretive little gestures,

each a probing, anxious kind of caress
of the new-grown patches of tender grass:
because it is friendly and the roses' red
might well, perhaps, present more of a threat,

perhaps something that will exceed again
what their hearts can hold, souls comprehend.
But for the time being, it remains hidden:
how quiet the grass is, how sweet to them.

Corpse-washing

They had become used to him. And yet when
the kitchen lamp was brought in and dimmed
and flared in the draught, the nameless man
was altogether unknown. These women,

bathing his neck, knowing nothing of his life,
began to make up a quite different one,
all the while washing. Then one had to cough
and she put the heavy, vinegar-soaked sponge

down on his face. Then the other woman
set her rough brush down too, needing to rest,
the wash-water dripping. His ghastly, stiff hand
wanted to make the whole house understand
he no longer needed to quench his thirst.

And he proved it. They turned back to the task
with a brief cough, the women bending closer,
more urgently, their stooping shadows cast
silent patterns across the wallpaper,

dipping and twisting as if trapped in a net,
till the washing of the corpse was complete.
Out beyond the curtainless window frame
stood pitiless night. And the one with no name
lay there naked, cleansed, left to legislate.

The Site of the Fire

As if bright autumn's dawn had caught sight of
and shunned what lay beyond the blackened
lime trees surrounding the house on the heath:
a new emptiness. Or one more playground

for children from God knows where to shout
amongst themselves, to play at pick up rags;
yet struck dumb, seeing the son of the house
making use of a long, forked branch to drag

a kettle, and blackened pots, a broken sieve,
from under the hot, half-burnt beams of the roof;
then with the look of one not telling the truth,
staring back as if to make them believe

in the thing that had once occupied this place.
For now it was gone, even to him, it seemed
more fantastical than the Pharaohs, as strange.
And he too, changed, as from a far-off land.

The Troupe

Paris

As if somebody quickly picked a bouquet:
Chance arranges their faces hastily,
separating these, pressing them close again,
seizing two far-off ones, not this nearby,

changing this for that, with a breath freshens,
ejecting a dog like a discarded weed,
lifting this limp one, then another threaded
head-first into place, through a crowd of stems,

and bound in, a fine detail, at the margin;
and reaching again, to shift, to make amends,
till there's hardly time enough to spring back,

for inspection, to the middle of the mat,
on which the glistening weightlifter now stands,
with all his powerful muscles bulging.

The Balcony

Naples

Above, on the iron-railed balcony,
pressed close, as if arranged by a painter,
gathered together as for a bouquet
of faces, smooth ovals, some much older,
more touching in evening's clarity,
more ideal, as if set there forever:

these sisters, leaning towards each other,
as if separated by vast distances,
hopelessly longing one for the other,
loneliness inclining to loneliness;

and their brother, serious and quiet,
withdrawn into himself, full of ability,
yet resembling his mother for a moment,
a softer look, unnoticed, in his eye;

and between them, gaunt and attenuated,
no longer true kin to these others,
the inscrutable mask of an old woman
who—as if she's already sinking down—
is propped by one hand, while the other,
more withered one is slack beside her gown,
as if its falling could not be halted,

and hangs there beside the face of the child,
who is their latest and pallid attempt,
yet is scored through by the balcony's rail,
as if undefined still, as if still in doubt.

Parrot Park

Jardin des Plantes, Paris

At the lawn's edge, under flowering Turkish lime trees,
on perches gently swung by their yearning for home,
the birds breathe, still conscious of their own countries,
which must be—though invisible here—still the same.

Strangers amongst this bustling green like a parade,
they preen, put on airs, feel themselves above it all,
with their spectacular beaks of jasper and jade,
they munch the grey feed, find it tasteless, let it fall.

Down below, the drab pigeons peck up what they drop,
while high above the mocking parrots take a bow,
perched between each almost empty, squandered trough.

Then back to glaring and sleeping, swaying to and fro,
absent-mindedly, with black tongues that love to lie,
they toy with their chains. Wait for witnesses to go by.

Encounter in the Avenue of Chestnuts

The instant he entered, the darkling green,
like a silk-lined cloak, closed coolly round him,
and he was just settling into it when,
at the other, far off, transparent end,

from green sunlight as through green panes of glass,
shone the white flare of a single figure
that remained for a long time in the distance,
and eventually, from the light's downpour,
swirling around every step, was cast

a bright shape-shifting, in motion towards him,
falling back shyly into the lit beyond.
Yet all at once the shadows deepened,
and there, up close, a pair of eyes, wide open,

in a clear, new face, with its lingering gaze
holding his own like that of a portrait,
for an instant, apart, once more, walking on:
at first, it was forever, and then gone.

Piano Practice

Summer drones on. Afternoon leaves her weary,
inhaling the freshness of her dress, confused,
and investing the compelling etude
with all her impatience for a reality

that might come tomorrow, or this evening,
or perhaps was there already, concealed;
and through tall windows that possessed everything,
she suddenly felt the parkland spoilt.

At that she broke off; gazed out, then, wringing
her hands, felt a yearning for a long book,
and angrily pushed the scented jasmine
further from her. Its perfume made her sick.

The Flamingos

Jardin des Plantes, Paris

Mirror images, as if by Fragonard,
could not convey their white and blushing red
any more vividly than if someone said,
of his girlfriend, 'Imagine her, laid there,

soft still with sleep.' Then up on to the green,
they stand around, balancing on pink stems,
side by side, blooming, as if in a flowerbed,
and, even more enticingly than Phryne,

seducing themselves; until they turn aside
to sink their pale eyes into downy feathers,
where black- and red-fruit colours lie concealed.

Now, an envy shrieks through the aviary;
they stretch, wondering, then one after another
stride off into the imaginary.

The Apple Orchard

Borgeby-Gård

Then come here just after the sun has set
to see evening's green deepen in the lawn;
is it not as if we had gathered it
within us, conserved it for a long time,

and now, from feeling, from recollection,
from new hope and half-forgotten joys,
still mingled with the darkness from within,
in our thoughts we scatter it before us

beneath these trees, as if drawn by Dürer,
bearing the weight of a hundred days' labour,
filling the overabundance of fruit,
each ministering, striving, yet patient,

as if that which, exceeding all measure,
may yet be lifted up and gathered in,
through a long life, if we willingly desire
increase in silence, this one simple thing.

Buddha in Glory

Centre of centres, core of all cores,
almond, self-enclosed, becoming sweeter:
all this, even to the furthest stars,
is the flesh of your fruit: hail what you are.

See, you feel nothing is clinging to you
any more; your hull, at the infinite,
where the powerful juices rise and flow.
And from outside, a radiance helps it,

for at the zenith your every sun spins
in full, incandescent splendour.
Yet within you, already, beginning to stir,
that which outlasts all suns.

FROM
REQUIEM
(1909)

Requiem for a Friend

I have my dead and I have let them go
and was astonished to see them so at ease
in being dead, so right, so soon at home,
so at odds with what we're told. Only you
return, brushing by me, lingering, now
tap something to make it sound, reveal
your presence. Do not deprive me of what
I'm slowly learning. I am right; you're wrong,
amiss to feel homesickness for anything
in this realm. We transform such things; they
are not here, but are reflected, in us,
in the very moment we encounter them.

    I thought you were further on. It troubles me
that *you* return, in error, you, who achieved
more transformation than any other woman.
That we were afraid when you died—no, more
that your sudden death broke blackly upon us
to sever the past from what was yet to come:
this is for us now to resolve, and this is
the task that we will always have before us.
But that *you* were frightened and, even now,
feel terror where terror makes no sense,
that you may have lost even the smallest
part of eternity, my friend, simply for this,

here, where nothing yet *is*; that, distracted
in endless space, distracted for the first time,
so failing to grasp the rising of infinite
natures as here you once did with all things.
That from the circling that swept you up,
the dumb gravity of some discontent
has dragged you back to gaugeable time:
this wakes me often like a thief in the night.
If I could simply say that you returned
out of kindness, or generosity,
or that you are secure and self-contained,
wandering here like a child, at liberty,
with no fear of what might afflict you...
But no. You plead. This is what lacerates
to the bone—it is what rasps like a saw.
Any reproach your ghost might bring me
in the night, however harsh, as I retreat
into my lungs, the workings of my guts,
into my heart's last, poorest chamber,
any reproach could not be as dreadful
as this pleading... What is it you want? ...

　　Tell me, must I travel? Did you forget
something, left in agony, and now it wants
to pursue you? Must I go to the land
you never saw, though you held it dear,
as if it composed one half of your senses?

　　I will sail its rivers. I will make landfall
and I will ask about its ancient customs.
I will talk with women in their doorways,

watching as they call their children home.
I will notice the way they wrap themselves
in their own landscape, even as they attend
to the old ways of fields and meadows.
I will ask to be brought before their king.
I'll bribe the priests to lead me to their most
powerful idol, to leave me there alone,
to turn away and close the temple gates.
And when I have learnt enough, only then
will I observe the animals, allowing
something of their elegant grace to slide
into my limbs. My wish will be to exist,
if only briefly, in their eyes, which hold,
then release me, calmly, without judgement.
From their gardeners, I will enquire what
they call the many flowers, so, returning,
I will carry with me a few remnants
of their hundreds of pleasing fragrances
in the little clay pots of their lovely names.
I will buy fruit there too—fruit, in which
the landscape, from earth to sky, lives once more.

    For you understood such things: ripe fruit.
You would display them in bowls before you,
would take the weight of each with colour.
You saw women the way you saw fruit.
And children you saw moulded from within
to the developing forms of their lives.
Finally, you saw even yourself as fruit,
eased yourself from your clothes and brought

yourself to a mirror, let yourself be seen,
yet your gaze remaining wide before it,
you did not say 'I am this', rather 'this is'.
At last, your sight, so cleared of curiosity,
unpossessing, of such true poverty,
no longer desired even yourself: holy.

This is how I want to recall you, finding
yourself in the mirror, deep within it,
yet far removed. So why return like this?
Why deny yourself? In the amber beads
round your neck, you want to persuade me,
there resides a weight even more profound
than that never to be found in the tranquil
heaven of paintings? Why show evil omens
in the way you stand? Why delineate
the contours of your body as lines on a palm
in which I can read nothing but destiny?

Come into the candlelight. I'm not afraid
to look the dead in the eye. When they come,
they have as much right as anything else
to rest and pause and linger in our gaze.

Come here. Let us be quiet for a while.
Look at this rose here on my writing desk;
the light around it—is it not as timid
as that around you? It too should not be here.
Outside, uninvolved with me, in the earth,
it should have gone on living, or died there.
Now it lasts. What is my awareness to it? ...

Don't be alarmed if I grasp it now—ah,
it wells up in me and cannot be helped,

yet I must, even if I am to die of it,
must understand you are here. And I do:
the way a blind man grasps a nearby thing.
I feel your fate—but I cannot name it.
Then let us lament that someone snatched you
from that mirror. Can you still weep?
You cannot. You transformed the urgency
and might of tears to the maturation
of your gaze and almost approached the point
of turning all sap within to potent being
so it might lift, swirling, balanced, blindly.
Then it was chance, one last time, chance
pulled you back from that far advance,
back into this world where sap holds sway.
It tore you, not all at once, a shred at first,
then, day by day, round this shred, there grew
the reality, swelling, weighing heavy,
and you had need of your whole self: then,
in need of yourself, you broke yourself up,
freed yourself slowly from what is decreed.
Then from the night-warm soil of your heart
you cleared debris, dug up the still-green seeds
from which your death was to germinate:
your death, rightly yours, to close out your life.
And you ate them, the kernels of your death,
like all the others, you swallowed the seeds
and they left a sweet aftertaste that you
had not expected, a sweetness on your lips,
you: already so sweet within your senses.

Oh, let us lament. Do you know how loath
your blood was to return when you called it
back from its incomparable circuiting?
How bewildered it was, taking up once more
the petty cycles of the body, how filled
with doubt, amazed, entering the placenta,
exhausted suddenly from its long return.
Yet you drove it on, urging it, dragging it
to the hearth as we drag a group of animals
to the altar, you wanted it happy there.
At last, you compelled it. It was content.
It ran to you, gave itself up. And you thought,
being used to quite different measures,
that this would not last very long; but you
were now within time and time is long, time
hurries on and time increases and time
is like a relapse into a chronic disease.

How short your life seems measured against
other hours, passed in silence, as you sat,
channelling the abundant energies
of your many futures for the new-bud child,
and that too was fate. Oh, painful labour!
Oh, labour beyond all strength! And you did it,
day after day, dragged yourself before it,
you pulled the lovely weft out of the loom,
re-wove all your threads to a new pattern:
still had the strength, at last, to celebrate.

When it was done you sought your reward,
like children when they have swallowed

bittersweet tea that will perhaps cure them.
You chose your reward, being, even then,
so far beyond all others that no one could
have imagined the reward to please you.
But you knew. Sitting up in the childbed,
you set before you a mirror which gave you
back entirely. Now all that was *you*,
and all *before*, while inside was deception,
the sweet lie of any woman who, smiling,
puts on her jewellery, rearranges her hair.

And so you died, as women used to die,
out of the warm house, an old-style passing,
the death of women in childbirth who want
to close themselves up again, yet cannot
since the ancient dark they have also brought
to the world returns, insists, and enters in.

Perhaps, after all, we should have summoned
wailing women? Those happy to lament
for money, those who can be paid to howl
through the long silence of the night for you.
How we need rituals! We do not have enough
such rituals, all talked out of existence.
So you have to return, dead, here, to me,
to grieve at our omission. You hear me wail?
Oh, I would fling my voice out like a cloak
across the shards of your death and then tug
till it has been torn to shreds and whatever
I have to say would then go shivering,
wrapped only in the tatters of that voice;

if grieving were enough. But I accuse too:
not the one who tore you from yourself
(I cannot find him; he is like the others)
but I accuse them all in this one, all men.

If sometimes the sense of being a child
stirs deep in me, something I never knew,
perhaps the purest part of childlikeness
from my childhood: I do not want to know it.
I want to shape an angel from it and fling
him skywards, high into the vanguard ranks
of shrieking angels to draw the gaze of God.

For already, this suffering has gone on
too long, none can bear it; it is too much
for any of us, this tangled suffering,
out of delusory love, dependent
on convention as much as habit, thinking
itself right to profit from what is wrong.
Where is the man with rights of possession?
Who can hold what cannot possess itself,
but can hardly, if joyfully, catch itself,
throw itself away like a child playing ball.
No more can a sea captain clasp the carved
image of victory on his ship's prow,
when the mysterious lightness of godhead
luffs her on into the bright ocean breeze;
no more can a man call back the woman
who departs, no longer conscious of us,
tracing the narrow ribbon of her life
quite safely, miraculously, she leaves:
unless his wish, his calling, is at fault.

For *this* is wrong, if anything is wrong:
not to enlarge the liberty of our loves
with all the freedom we find within us.
When we love, we must practise only this:
let each other go, for holding on comes
easily, is not something we need to learn.

Are you still here? In which corner are you?
You had such an understanding of all this
as you passed through life, so capable
and open to it as each day's dawning.
That women suffer: love is to live alone,
that artists sometimes feel this in their work,
that they must transform where they love.
You set about both and both live in what
fame steals from you now to misrepresent.
Ah, unnoticed, quiet, you drew your beauty
into yourself as one furls a bright flag
come the grey dawn of a new working day,
asking for nothing but sustained work—
left unfinished now, ever incomplete.

If you are still here, if in this darkness
there is still a place in which your spirit
shivers faintly with the shallow sound waves
that one solitary voice, at night, alone,
excites in the airs of a lofty room:
then hear me, help me. See, the way we slip
suddenly back from our every advance,
unknowing, to what we never desired;

there, as in dreams, we become entangled
and may die there, without ever waking.
None went further. Anyone who has raised
their blood to a work, to lengthy labour,
may find, perhaps, it cannot be upheld,
it falls under its own weight, is worthless.
For somewhere there is an old enmity
between the life lived and great work to be done.
That I can see this and say this: help me.

   Don't come back. If you can bear it, remain
dead with the dead. They have their own tasks.
But help me, if it does not distract you,
for sometimes what is furthest helps: in me.

UNCOLLECTED POEMS
(1913–1922)

The Spanish Trilogy

I

From this cloud, look: obscuring the star
so wildly, hiding what was there——(and from me),
from mountains beyond, now clasping night
for a while, and the night winds——(and from me),
from this stream on the valley floor, a glint,
a jagged tear in the sky caught in it——(and from me);
to make from me, and from all this, to make
one thing, Lord: from me and the feeling
of the flock as it finds its way back to the fold,
breathing acceptance of the vast and dark
withdrawal of the world——from me and each light
in the darkness of the many houses, Lord:
to make one thing; and from strangers, for there
is no one here I know, and from me, from me,
to make *one* thing; from all now lost in sleep,
from the old, unknown men at the hospice,
in their beds, with their meaningful coughing,
from children drowsing on such strange breasts,
from countless uncertainties and always from me,
nothing but me and from what I do not know,
make the one thing, Lord Lord Lord, the thing,
the earthly-worlding that is like a meteor,
gathering no more than the sum of flight,
only to weigh in at nothing but arrival.

II

Why must a man walk out and take to himself
strange things—as perhaps a porter must do,
from stall to stall, with the market basket
being loaded with strange items, more and more,
and he cannot say: Lord, why this banquet?

Why must a man stand here like a shepherd,
so exposed to the excess of influence,
so involved in space crammed with occurrence,
who—simply leaning by a tree in the landscape—
would achieve his destiny, no more to do.
And yet, in his too open gaze, he has none
of the silent comforting of the flock—
nothing but world, world in every up-glance,
in his every inclination, world. Because what
others like to hear pierces him like a music,
drives blindly, harshly, through his blood and gone.

Then he rises at night, and he finds the call
of a bird outside is already within him
and he feels bold as he gathers the stars
gravely into his face—Oh, nothing like the one
who readies such a night for his beloved
and then pampers her with his heartfelt heaven.

III

That I may yet, returned to the throng of the city,
its entangling clamour, and to the chaos
of traffic on every side, yet still quite alone,
above its dense confusions, may I yet recall
the sky, even then, the earth's mountain rim
on which the flock moved, all heading home.
Let my courage be like a rock,
and the shepherd's day's work within my grasp,
strolling, tanned by the hot sun, with a stone,
precisely thrown, mending the fraying flock.
His pace is slow, not easy, his body pensive,
yet he stands magnificent. A god, even now
secretly taking this form, would not be diminished.
Pausing, by turns, he moves on, like the day,
and the shadows of the clouds
are passing through him as if the wide expanse
is slowly thinking thoughts on his behalf.

Let him be whoever you wish. Like a flickering nightlight
within the lamp's mantle, I place myself in him.
A flare grows steady. Death
may more easily find its way.

Raising Lazarus

So, it was important to one or another,
for they wanted signs without any doubt.
Yet he dreamt how—for Mary or Martha—
it ought to have been enough they accept
he *could* do such things. But none had faith.
All exclaimed: Lord, why come *now*, why here?
And so, he determined to undertake
a thing forbidden to the peace of Nature.
Angry. His eyes almost shut, all but blind,
he asked the way to the grave. In agony.
To them, he was weeping—or so it seemed—
as they gathered, full of curiosity.
Even as he walked, still filled with horror
at this dreadful, frivolous experiment,
within him a great conflagration flared,
suddenly blazing out in argument
against their petty sense of distinction,
that life and death stood clear and plain,
so he felt enmity in every limb
as he hoarsely instructed: Lift the stone!
A voice cried out: he must stink, for sure,
(he had lain there four days). Even so, he
stood firmly, suffused with the gesture
of beckoning which rose in him—heavily,

heavy, the hand moved (no hand ever stirred
more slowly, then it lifted a little more)
until there it stood, glistening in the air,
and clenching slowly, it was like a claw:
for now, suddenly, he feared all the dead,
in a flood, might seize the chance to return
through the broken vacuum of the tomb,
where, larva-like, it rose from where it lay…
but just one single form stood, crookedly,
in the light: and they could all see the way
Life, though yet vague and indeterminate,
took it back once more, settling it into place.

The Spirit Ariel

after reading Shakespeare's THE TEMPEST

Once, somewhere, he was set free with the jolt
that you too, as a young man, once suffered,
torn into greatness, far beyond all regard.
Then he grew willing, and see: now he serves,
and with each task is eager to be freed.
And half utterly majestic, half ashamed,
you explain to him, for this thing or for that,
he is still required and, ah, relate once more
how much you have helped. Yet you feel, yourself,
how all that is held back, in detaining him,
is lost to the air. How sweet, almost tempting,
to let him go—and then no more conjuring,
but to be subject to fate, as the others are,
to be aware that his easy friendship
is no longer strained, is no more obliged,
a superfluity to this breathing's space,
at work in the element without a thought.
Henceforth, dependent, no longer endowed
with the gift to shape the dull mouth to cries
to which he stooped. Powerless, ageing, poor,
yet breathing *him* like some unfathomable,
far-flung scent which serves finally to make
the invisible complete. Smiling, that you
could summon him, still feeling quite at home

in such acquaintance. Perhaps, weeping too,
when you remember how he loved you, yet still
wished to leave, both, always in the same moment.

(And have I yet let go? Now this man scares me,
reverting to Duke once more. How gently
he draws the wire through his own head to hang
himself up alongside the others, then asks
for the crowd's indulgence... What an epilogue
of power, achieved—set aside—to stand there
with no strength but his own, 'which is most faint'.)

The Vast Night

Often, I wondered at you, at a window begun only
    yesterday,
stood in awe of you. As yet, the new
city was as if denied me, the unpersuaded landscape
darkened as if I did not exist. The nearest objects
made no effort to be intelligible. The street
surged up to the lamp post: I saw it was strange.
Across the way—a room, sympathetic, vivid in the light—
already, I took part; they knew it, closed the shutters.
Stood. And then a child, crying. I was conscious of mothers
in nearby houses, what they are capable of—I knew
the inconsolable reasons for weeping.
Or there was a voice, singing, reaching out
beyond expectation, or an elderly man coughing below,
full of reproach as if his body were in the right,
rather than the gentler world. Then the hour struck,
but I counted too late, and it slipped from me—
like a boy, a newcomer, allowed to play at last,
but he cannot catch the ball, is hopeless at games
the others play with each other so easily,
so he stands there, looks away—to where?—so I stood,
and suddenly, *you* were with me, playing, I knew you, grown-
    up
night, I marvelled at you. Where the towers

raged, where, with its averted fate,
the city stood round me, where unfathomable mountains
ranged against me, and strangeness, hungering,
in narrowing circles, closed in on the chance flickering
of my feelings—then it was that you, great one,
with no trace of shame, acknowledged me. Your breath
swept over me. Your smile, spanning a vast
solemnity, entered into me.

'You, beloved, lost'

You, beloved, lost
in advance, never arrived—
I do not know what sounds are sweet to you.
No longer do I try to discern you in the waves
of what is to come. All the vast
images within me—the far-off, experienced landscapes,
cities and towers and bridges and the un-
anticipated turns in the road,
and the grandeur of those lands
once pervaded by the lives of gods:
all rise in me, signifying
you, yet elusive as ever.

Ah, the gardens are you,
I beheld them, oh, with so much
hopefulness. An open window
in the country house—and you almost approached
me there, pensively. I discovered back streets
you had just walked along
and sometimes, in crowded shops, the mirrors,
still dizzy with your passing, and startled, shot back
my own too-sudden image. Who knows if the same
bird did not sing through each of us,
yesterday, separately, in the dusk?

Turning Point

The way from inner intensity to greatness leads through sacrifice—RUDOLF KASSNER

For a long time, he achieved it by looking.
Stars fell to their knees
before his grappling upward glance.
Or he gazed, kneeling,
and the whiff of his urgency
exhausted the divine
so that it smiled upon him, sleeping.

He stared at towers in such a way
as to frighten them:
rebuilt them again, suddenly, in a moment!
Yet how often the landscape,
overburdened by the day,
rested in his quiet perception in the evening.

Animals stepped confidently,
grazing, into his open look,
and the captive lions
stared into it as if into incomprehensible freedom;
birds flew directly
through its accommodating space; flowers
gazed back into it,
wide-eyed as children.

And the rumour that here was someone who saw
moved the obscured,
the more uncertainly seen:
it stirred women.

Looking—for how long?
For how long, already profoundly lacking,
a beseeching at the root of his gaze?

When he, the waiting one, sat somewhere strange—the hotel's
distracted, averted room
around him, sullenly, and in the avoided mirror
the same room again,
and later, from the tormenting bed,
once again, there:
there, in the air, a deliberation
beyond comprehension, in consideration
of his still-palpable heart,
concerning his heart which was felt, nevertheless,
through the aching, buried body,
a deliberation and judgement:
that it had no love.

(And so denied him further blessings.)

For there is, you see, a limit to looking.
And the world, so looked upon,
wants to flourish in love.

Work of the eyes is over with,
turn now to heart-work
on these images within you, those imprisoned ones; for you
overpowered them: but now, you do not know them.
Behold, inner man, your inner woman,
this, first won
of a thousand natures,
this, as yet, merely achieved,
not yet ever beloved creation.

To Hölderlin

To linger, even amongst what is most familiar,
is not given to us; from images fulfilled,
the spirit rushes abruptly to those yet to be filled:
there are no lakes until eternity. Here, falling
is the best we do. From the mastered emotion,
flung down into the yet-to-be-guessed-at, then on.

To you, glorious one, conjurer, the urgent image
was an entire life—and when you uttered it,
your line fell shut like fate, with a death
even in the mildest, and still you entered it; and yet,
the god ahead of you brought you out and beyond.

Oh, you roaming spirit, most shifting! How all the others
loiter in lukewarm poems, comfortable, dwell
too long in cramped similes. Taking part. Only you
move like the moon. And below, brightening, darkening,
your nightscape, that hallowed, startled landscape
you feel in leave-taking. No one ever
surrendered it more nobly, gave it back to the whole
so intact, less marred by need. So too,
you played, holy, through years you no longer reckoned,
with that infinite joy, as if it were not within
but lay about you, belonging to no one, on the earth's

tender grasses, let drop there by godlike children.
Ah, what the very greatest wish for, you, undesiring,
laid down brick after brick: it stood. Even its downfall
left you unbewildered.

Why, after such a life, eternal one, do we still distrust
the earthly? Rather than learning in earnest,
from the provisional, emotions
for whatever inclination awaits us, in prospect, in space?

FROM
DUINO ELEGIES
(1923)

The First Elegy

Who, if I cried out, would hear me amongst the ranks
of the angels? Even if one of them clasped me
suddenly to his heart, I would wither in the face
of his more fierce existence. For their beauty
is really nothing but the first stirrings of a terror
we are just able to endure and are astonished
at the way it elects, with such careless disdain,
to let us go on living. Every angel is terrifying.
    And so I hold back, swallow back the bird-call
of black grief that would burst from me.
Ah, who is it we can turn to for help? Not angels.
Not other people. Even the knowing creatures
already dumbly see we do not feel at home
in our interpretations of the world, though there is,
perhaps, a specific tree on a hillside we settle on,
over and over. Or yesterday's stroll remains,
through the usual streets—the comforting loyalty
of a habit that took a liking to us,
that moved in and now will not leave us alone.
    Oh, and the night. Night with a wind that comes
as if filled with infinity and gnaws at our faces.
This is what awaits every one of us—
the looked-for, tender disenchantment of the night—
so hard for hearts alone to bear. Though is it

any easier for lovers? They make use of each other
to hide what they know must otherwise come.

Do you not see this *yet*? Fling this emptiness
out of your arms, back into the spaces
into which we breathe and suddenly the birds
will feel the more expansive air, will sense it,
perhaps, with a more fervent flying.

Yes—the springtimes needed you. There were stars
waiting to be seen by you. A wave rolled
to your feet in the past, or as you strode
beneath half-shuttered windows, the bowed violin
leant itself to you. All this was your mission.
But were you up to it? Were you not more often
distracted by anticipation, as if everything
about you was there only to herald a beloved?
(Oh, but where would you keep her—what with
strange thoughts looming in and out of your head,
from dawn to dark, so often staying the night?)
Rather, if desire tempts you, sing of the lovers,
those famous ones, though even their love is
not immortal enough, those—you almost envy
them this—forsaken, abandoned and unrequited,
who have so much more loving within them
than those who are satisfied. Begin, like them,
and begin again the eternal task of praising!
Remember this: the hero lives for ever.
His death is no more than a pretext for being,
his latest birth—whereas lovers are withdrawn

back into Nature, sapped and spent, as if
it had no strength left to create their like again.
Have you imagined the love of Gaspara Stampa?
Recalled it so intensely that any girl—deserted
by her lover—might emulate her fine example
and might say to herself: Let me be like her!
Because is it not time this oldest of heartaches
finally bore us some fruit? Is it not time,
though still loving, we learnt to wrench ourselves
free of the beloved and, though trembling,
endure as the arrow endures the tensed bowstring,
becomes something *more* than itself in the leap
of release? For our point of rest is nowhere.

Voices. Voices. My heart, listen, now listen,
as only the saints have done before you
until a gigantic calling lifted them bodily
from the ground and they rose, impossibly,
still kneeling, still unaware, so intently they listened.
Not that you could bear *God's* voice—far from it.
So then listen to the wind's, its ceaseless
message risen from silence, bringing whispers
of all who died young. Did their fate not come to you,
quietly, to speak, as you stepped into churches
in Rome or Naples? Or did some sublime epitaph
not impose on you? Remember, so recently,
that day: the plaque in Santa Maria Formosa?
What they ask of me is gently to shake off
the sense of injustice that still troubles their deaths

and sometimes hinders them a little, holds them
back in the onward process of their soul.

It is true enough, of course, no longer to live
on earth is strange, to abandon customs
yet barely mastered, not to interpret the roses
and other auspicious things, not give them meaning
in a human future. No longer to be as we have
always been, in those endlessly anxious hands—
to leave even our name behind us as a child
leaves off playing with a broken toy. Strange,
no longer to know desires desired—strange
to witness the involvement of all things lost
suddenly, each drifting away singly into space.
And truly, to be dead is hard, so full of making
up lost ground, till little by little we can find
a trace of eternity. Yet, the living are wrong
to credit such distinctions so clearly:
angels (it is said) are often never quite sure
whether they pass amongst the living or the dead,
since through both these realms, and forever,
eternity's flood tumbles all the ages and in both
their cries are drowned out by its roar.

In the end, the young-dead do not need us:
they are weaned off the earth mildly, as a child
will outgrow the mother's breast. But we,
who long for such great mysteries, we, for whom
sorrow is often the path on which we progress—

can we exist without them? Is the old myth
really nonsense? The one of the mourning of Linus,
how music first broke on the barren wilderness;
how, in the startled space left gaping by the loss
of a boy like a god, emptiness rang as never before
with what holds us rapt, comforts now and can help.

The Second Elegy

Every angel is terrifying. And yet, alas, I go on
singing to you in the knowledge of what you are,
you all but deadly birds of the soul.
Where are the days of Tobias, when one of these
most radiant creatures stood at the simple doorway
ready to travel, in part disguised, and not
so frightening (a young man, in fact, like the one
peering curiously out to see who was there).
If the archangel bent down now, dangerously
bent from behind the spread of stars, took one step
towards us, we would be beaten to death
by our own high-beating heart. Who are you?

Perfection's firsts, creation's pampered favourites,
the peaks and summits we look to, where they
redden in the first touch of the created world—
spilt pollen of flowering Godhead, knots of light,
passageways, stairs, thrones, spaces of life,
the blazoned shields of bliss, tumults of ecstasy
and as suddenly, solely—*mirrors*, scooping
up that flood of beauty that pours from them
and redirecting it back into themselves.

For we, even as we feel, evaporate in the act
of breathing ourselves out and beyond,
ember after ember, we burn away to nothing.
We give off an ever-diminishing scent.
Though somebody might come to say, 'Yes!
You are in my blood now. This room, the whole
of spring filled with your presence…' What's the use?
He cannot preserve us. We still disappear
in him or around him. Even the truly beautiful—
who holds them? Nothing but appearance
continually rises and departs in their faces.
Like a morning dew, where it rises from the grass,
so vanishes what is ours—it is like heat ascending
from uncovered dishes. Oh, that smile there!
Where is it going? Those up-glancing eyes
that propel a warm but forever ebbing wave
through the heart—alas, that is what we *are*.
The space beyond us, into which we continually
dissipate, does it come to taste of us at all?
Do angels take back into themselves only
what is theirs, only what has streamed from them,
or do they, as if mistakenly, take in a trace
of what we are? Are we mixed into their features
as subtly as that vague look you see pass
across the faces of pregnant women? Of course,
they do not notice, occupied in the whirling
reinvigoration of themselves. (How could they notice?)

Yet lovers, if they knew how, might articulate
wonders in the night air, though it seems
all things intend to obscure us. Look—trees *exist*.
The houses we live in continue to stand. Only we
pass away like air traded for air and everything
conspires to maintain silence about us, perhaps,
half out of shame, half out of unspeakable hope.

Lovers—you who find satisfaction in each other—
I ask you about us. You hold one another,
but where is the proof? Look—sometimes my hands
know comfort in each other. Or sometimes I shelter
my worn face in them. Then I am in touch
with some slight sensation. Yet who'd dare step
into existence for that? Lovers—do you not grow
ever more present in each other's passion until,
overwhelmed, you beg—'No *more*!'—
you, who at the touch of the other's hands swell,
fill out to such abundance like grapes
in a fine vintage—you, who sometimes vanish,
though only in moments the other is so fully present—
I am asking you about us. I know it's bliss for you
to touch, since every caress conserves the place
on a lover's body you cover so tenderly—
it cannot be lost. You sense a permanence beneath it.
You almost promise eternity in your embrace.
And yet, once you have survived the terrors
of first glances, of daydreaming at the window,
of a first walk, that *once*, together on through

the gardens, then *do* you remain the same forever?
When you lift one another, raise each other to drink
the full draught, mouth on mouth—oh, strange,
the way each drinker grows distant from the act.

Were you not astonished at the restraint of human
gestures on Attic stelae? Wasn't love and parting
laid so gently on their shoulders they appeared
to be made of material other than this world?
Remember how lightly the hands pressed, though there
was great strength in the torsos? Those people knew
such self-control: 'We go only so far—this touching
each other—*this* is ours—as for the gods, they impose
on us more fiercely, but that must be for the gods.'

If only we too could discover such a pure,
contained and human place, our own fertile stretch
between river and rock, since, as theirs did long ago,
our heart always exceeds us, and we can no longer
pursue it by contemplating images inclined
to soothe, nor is it any use gazing at god-like forms
more magnificently capable of restraint.

from The Third Elegy

It is one thing to sing the beloved, quite another,
alas, to invoke the hidden, guilty river-god
of the blood. Take a young lover—what does he,
whom she may know as yet only remotely,
what does he know of that lord of desire
who often, breaking out of his solitude,
and even before she has the chance to soothe him,
acts as if she were nothing to him—a god, ah,
raising its head, dripping, unfathomable, urgent,
turning the night over to endless uproar.
Oh, this is the Neptune inhabiting our blood,
the god who wields such terrifying weapons!
His dark breath blows through the windings
of a conch! Listen to where the night begins
to gape and hollow! Oh, you stars—the lover's
desire for the face of his beloved, does it not
rise first from you? Doesn't his deepest response
to her pure face come from the pure, bright stars?

Not from you, alas, and nor was it his mother
who so tensed up the bow of his brows
in such anticipation. Nor was it for you, girl,
despite all your sensitivity to his presence—
no, it was not for your lips, particularly,

that his lips pursed so fruitfully.
Do you really think you could have shaken him so
with your gentle arrival, you who move
as delicately as a breeze at dawn. Of course,
you did startle his heart indeed, but really
it was these older horrors, plunged to his depths
at your touch. Call him... but you cannot quite
call him away from those dark companions.
He *wants* to escape them, of course, and he does.
Then, relieved, he nestles into the seclusion
of your loving heart, takes hold to begin himself—
but did he ever really begin himself?
Mother, *you* made him small. It was you began him.
He was so new to you, over his new-born brows
you bent a friendly world, shut out the strange one.
Oh, where are all those years when you used
your slim form and simply stood in the way
of seething chaos? How much you hid from him!
The suspect chamber of darkness you made
harmless and, out of the refuge of your heart,
you stirred more humanity into his night-space.
And in the darkness, you did not set a light,
but rather deployed your own presence within it
and there let it shine like a companion.
There was no creak your smile could not explain.
It was as if you had always known *when* the boards
would do that... And he listened to you
and knew himself soothed. You stood over him
so tenderly till the long-cloaked figure of his fate

retreated beyond the wardrobe and his future
restlessness took the shape of a folded curtain,
though all this was easy postponement.

And as he lay there, himself, relieved in the sweetness
of the gentle world you had conjured before him,
dissolving under drowsy eyelids towards sleep,
he *seemed* protected... but *inside* who could divert
or forestall the oncoming flood of his origins?
Ah! there *was* no precaution in the sleeper!
Sleeping, but dreaming, and that feverishly—
how he let himself go, he, the new one, shy one,
tangled in the spreading tendrils of inner events,
already entwined into patterns of choking
undergrowth, threaded by hunting bestial shapes.
How he submitted to it! Loved! How he loved
his inwardness! His inner wilderness!
The primal forest within, where his heart shone
like a beacon, pale green amongst the decay.
He loved it. And left it. Went down through
his own roots and out to the point of origin
where his little birth seemed an anachronism.
He waded deeper, deeper, still loving it,
to ancient blood, towards ravines, where terrors
lay in wait, gorged still with his own fathers,
and each horror knew him, winked in complicity.
Oh yes, the horrors smiled...
You, his mother, had hardly ever smiled with such
tenderness, so how could he resist loving

what had smiled at him? Yet he loved it even
before he knew you, since it was already dissolved
in the waters that buoyed him in your belly.

[...]

My dear girl, all *this* long preceded you.

And as for yourself, how could you have known
that you stirred prehistory in your lover?
What passion was it welled from the long-dead
in him? What women were there who hated you?
What men of darkness did you rouse in young veins?
What dead children reached their arms to you?
Oh, gently, gently, then! Let him watch you
at some steady, everyday task—lovingly, lead him
close up to the garden, give him whatever might
outweigh the nights...

                Hold him back...

from *The Fourth Elegy*

Oh, trees of life, when does your winter come?
We are not attuned, not at one, we lack the instinct
of migrant birds. Late, we get left standing—
we launch ourselves abruptly into the wind,
only to go plummeting down into waters
that do not care for us. At once, we feel ourselves
both wither and flower. Somewhere else, lions
roam unaware of any weakness in their majesty.

But for us, as we focus on one thing, we feel
already the pull of another. Conflict is always
our companion. Even those in love, are they
not always confronting each other's limits
though promised space, good hunting, a home?
    It is as if—in a quick sketch—all the effort
has gone to ready a background that allows us
to see precisely and yet still we cannot grasp
the real contour of our feelings, and we know
only the pressures that shape us from outside.

[…]

The Fifth Elegy

dedicated to Frau Hertha Koenig

But tell me, who *are* they, these drifters,
even more transient than we are, wrung out from the start
by some relentless will—and for *whose* sake?
Still, it wrings them and bends them,
slings and swings them, tosses them up
and catches them again,
and they tumble as if through oiled and slippery air
to stamp the threadbare carpet,
worn thin by their feet, their constant leaping
on to a carpet cut loose in the universe,
laid out here like a plaster
as if the suburban sky had wounded the earth.
                          And barely discernible,
yet upstanding and unmistakably displayed,
the capital D of Destiny… the unrelenting grip of it,
dallying with them, rolls even the toughest
and plays with them the way Augustus the Strong
would crush tin plates at his table.

Ah, and around this mid-point
gathers the rose of those who look on:
they bloom and fall away from this pounding pestle,
this pistil fertilized by the kicked-up dust
of its own pollen, though it can bear

only a joyless, false fruit—
the witless, gawping faces,
the glazed veneer and vacant smirk of boredom.

There—the shrivelled-up, wrinkled weightlifter—
an old man who now only beats a drum,
so shrunken in his baggy skin it looks big enough
to have once held *two* of him, the other
already laid in a graveyard and he, the lone survivor,
deaf and at times growing a little
confused in his widowed skin.

Yet there is the youth, the man, who might be
the offspring of a neck and a nun: bulging, strapping,
full of muscles and innocence.

Oh, you—
once given over to a grief when it was still small,
given as a plaything,
during one of its long convalescences...

Then you, who drop down a hundred times a day,
with the kind of bruising only unripened
fruit knows, out of the tree
of your collaborative efforts (which in moments
run through spring summer autumn faster than water),
you fall down thud on the grave:
sometimes, in a momentary pause, a tender look
to your seldom-affectionate mother,

trying to establish itself in your face—
but no, your body overpowers it,
that shy face you scarcely attempt… And again,
the man claps his hands for your leap and before
a pain can grow any sharper,
or closer to your galloping heart, you feel
a stinging in the soles of your feet
rushing ahead of the real cause of pain
and chasing a pair of smarting, quick tears into your eyes.
And yet, blindly,
that smile…

Angel—oh, pluck it, gather its small-flowering, healing herb.
Conjure a vase and preserve it. Set it there with the other
pleasures *not* yet open to us and give it
a precious jar and praise it
with a bold and flowing inscription:

> *Subrisio Saltat*

And then you, my lovely one,
past whom the sweetest of pleasures have swept
in silence. Perhaps the fringes of your costume
are happy for you,
or does its green silk, its metallic sheen,
stretched across your firm young breasts,
feel itself so infinitely spoilt
it wants for nothing?
You—
constantly, yet differently, weighed in the swaying

177

scales, performing with the blank indifference
of fruit displayed to the public,
before the push and shove of shoulders.

Where, oh, *where* is the place—I have it in my heart—
where they were not *able*, where they fell off
each other like rutting animals,
poorly paired—
where the weights were still too ponderous,
where the plates wobbled off poles
still being twirled in vain…

And suddenly, in this laborious nowhere—
suddenly, in this inexpressible place where the pure Too-little
is inexplicably translated, switching,
into the slick Too-much:
where the mass of intractable numbers
resolves, at last, and to nothing.

Squares, oh, square in that infinite showplace,
Paris—where *Madame Lamort*, the milliner,
twists and winds the unquiet ways of the world,
those endless ribbons from which she makes
these loops and ruches, rosettes and flowers and artificial fruits,
all dyed with no eye for the truth,
but to daub the cheap winter hats of fate.

. . . .

Angel! If there were some place we did not know of,
and there, on a carpet impossible to describe,
lovers could show what they cannot here,
the bold and high figures of their hearts' swinging,
the towering of their pleasure,
ladders for a long while standing on no solid ground,
but tremblingly leant only into the other's leaning,
and there, they could *perform* all this,
before spectators crowded round them,
the silent and innumerable dead:

    Would these then throw down their last, forever hoarded,
ever-hidden, unknown to us, eternally valid
coins of happiness before the, at last,
truly smiling pair, there, on the quenched
carpet?

The Sixth Elegy

Fig tree, how long has it been important to me,
the way you almost wholly skip blossoming,
and press pure mystery, quite unheralded,
into early-setting fruit. Like the pipe in a fountain,
your curved branches drive sap down, then up,
to spring, almost without waking from sleep,
to the bliss of the sweetest performance.
See—like the god entering the swan.

                ...Yet we linger too long,
ah, we glory in flowering, already betrayed
by the time we arrive at the long-awaited heart
of our final fruit. In only a few does the urge
to action rise so powerfully they stand ready,
at once, hearts brimming and aglow, before
the temptation to bloom, like a tender night air,
touches their young mouths, brushes their eyelids:
perhaps these are heroes, alongside those chosen
for an early demise, those whose veins
are twisted differently by the gardener, death.
These plunge on, run before their own smiles,
like the horses in the bas-relief carving at Karnak
that gallop on ahead of the triumphant king.

How strangely alike: the hero and the young dead.
Permanence does not concern him. His way of life

is one of ascent, continually setting out towards
the ever-shifting constellation of constant danger.
Few could find him there. But Fate, which to us
retains its dark obscurity, with him grows
inspired and sings him forwards into the storm
of his onrushing world. I hear of no one like *him*.
All at once, I am run through by his darkened
sound as it is carried to me on the streaming air.

Then, how I would like to hide from that longing:
oh, to be, to be a boy again with life yet to come,
to sit in the future's embrace, to read of Samson,
how his mother at first bore nothing, then everything.

Was he not already a hero within you, mother?
Did his own imperious choosing not begin inside?
Thousands brewed in the womb, wanting to be *him*.
But see: he grasped, let go—he chose and won out.
And when he shattered pillars, in that moment
he burst from the world of your body into this more
straitened one, where again he chose, he won out.
Oh, mothers of heroes, springs of those torrential rivers!
You, rifts into which, from the heart's high rim,
plunge grief-stricken girls, your son's future sacrifices.

    For when the hero went storming through
love's stations, each heart beating for his sake
served only to lift him higher, pushed him beyond
and, turned away, he stood at the end of all smiles—
something quite other.

from The Seventh Elegy

Then no more wooing, enough of this courting,
your voice has outgrown it; make that the burden
of your call, though you might cry out pure
as a bird when the stirring of the season lifts him
and he almost forgets he is a troubled creature,
not just a single heart flung towards cheerfulness,
to the embrace of heaven. Like him, even then,
you would still be wooing—so your unseen lover
would hear you, the silent one whose response
stirs slowly, in listening to you, as she warms
her passionate response to your bolder passion.

Oh, and spring would conceive it—there's no place
would fail to respond to such a proclamation.
At first, small notes would be as questionings,
intensified in the surrounding stillness
of the pure and affirming day. Then up steps,
the flight of calls, to the dreamt-of temple
of the future—then a trill of water, a jet, a rising
fountain, already embracing its tumbling down
in a game of promises… And soon, the summer.

[…]

Simply being here is glorious! *You* understood that,
you girls, even you who appeared so deprived
and in decline—you, in the dirtiest alleys of the city,
festering there or laid wide open to filth.
For each of you had an hour—or perhaps not
even an hour, a barely measurable moment
between whiles—when you felt a sense
of the destined shape of all things. Everything.
Your veins grew awash with it. But we so easily
forget what our laughing neighbour neither
affirms nor envies in us. For ourselves,
we want to make it visible—though the most
evident happiness goes unrecognized,
unless we can transform it—and that is within.

The world is nowhere, beloved, if not within.
Our life passes in transformation. The external world
is forever dwindling to nothing: where once
there stood a solid and lasting house,
now a dreamt-up construction straddles our path
and seems to belong entirely to the realm
of conception, as if it still stood in the brain.
The spirit of the age has engineered for itself
vast reservoirs of power, though they are formless
as the straining energy it draws from all things.
Temples are no longer known. It is we who
secretly conserve these extravagances of the heart.
Yes—where one still stands, a thing once prayed to,

worshipped, knelt before—it holds, as it is,
and it passes into the outwardly invisible.
Many no longer see it, so they miss the chance
to build it again, to build it *within* themselves,
with pillars and with statues, yet greater still.

Every stifled turning of the world discovers
the disinherited who do not possess their past,
nor what is yet to come. For even the next moment
is far off from man. Yet *we* should not become
confused by this, rather strengthened in preserving
the still-recognizable form… This once *stood*
amongst mankind, amidst ever-destructive fate,
in the middle of Not-Knowing-Where, it stood
as if enduring and it drew down the stars from
their secured heaven. Angel—to *you* I will show it,
there! In your vision it will stand, finally now
upright and rescued at last. Columns, gateways,
the Sphinx, the up-striving of the grey cathedral
in a city that is vanishing or is foreign to us.

Was this not miraculous? Marvel! Angel! We *are*
all this! We are—oh, great one—will you proclaim
what we can achieve? My own breath is too weak
for such praise! So we have not, after all this,
failed to make use of these generous spaces,
these spaces of *ours* (how frighteningly immense
they must be as thousands of years have passed
and still they do not overflow with feelings).

But a tower was great, was it not? Oh, angel, it was—
great, even set beside you? Chartres was great—
and music reached higher still, passing beyond us.
Even a girl in love, alone by a window at night...
did she not reach to your knee—?
                              Do *not* think I am wooing.
Angel, even if I were, you would not come.
For my call is always filled with leaving and against
such a powerful current you cannot advance.
My calling is like an outstretched arm.
And my hand, held open and reaching high
to grasp is, in fact, lifted before you,
splayed as if to ward off and warn
the ungraspable, far above.

from The Eighth Elegy

dedicated to Rudolph Kassner

With all its eyes, Creation looks on the Open.
Only ours seem to be turned backwards
and they appear to lay traps all around it,
as if to prevent its breaking free.
What *is* really out there we only know
by looking to the countenance of creatures.
For we take a young child and force it
to turn round, to see shapes and forms,
and not the Open that is so deep in the face
of an animal. Free from death.
Alone, *we* see it. The freed creature's doom
stands behind it and ahead lies God
and, when it begins to move, its movement
is through an eternity like a wellspring.

    Even for a single day, *we* do not have
that pure space before us into which flowers
endlessly bloom. We face always World
and never Nowhere without the No:
that unsurveyed purity we might breathe
and *know* without limit and not desire.
In such a stillness, a child may lose itself,
but then is shaken from it. Or someone
dies and *becomes* it. So close to death
we do not see so much of death, but look *out*

perhaps with the greater animal gaze.
Lovers—were it not for their loved ones
obstructing their view—may come close to it
and are amazed... As if by some mistake,
it opens to them, there, beyond the other...
But neither can slip past the beloved
and World rushes back before them.
Forever turned towards the created, we see
in it only reflections of the free realm
that we darken with our very presence.
Or it happens, an animal, mutely, quietly,
looks up, stares us through and through.
We call this Fate: to be opposed to World
forever and nothing else, only opposite.

[...]

And we are spectators: always, everywhere,
we face all this, never seeing beyond it!
It spills from us. We arrange it.
It falls to pieces. We arrange again.
We ourselves fall to pieces.

Who has twisted us this way round,
so that, no matter what we do, always,
we are in the position of one leaving? Just as,
on the last possible hill from which he can
glimpse his whole valley for one last time,
he turns, he pauses there, he lingers—
and so we live on, forever bidding goodbye.

The Ninth Elegy

Why—when the span of our life could be spent
happily as laurel, that bit darker than all
the other green, with tiny waves on every leaf edge
(like the smile of a breeze)—why then
the need to be human and, avoiding fate,
why keep longing for fate? ...

                     Oh, *not* because happiness *exists*,
that hasty profit we snatch from impending loss.
Not for curiosity's sake, nor as practice for the heart,
which could as well *exist* as laurel...

But truly because being here is so much—because
everything in this fleeting world seems to need us,
calls to us strangely. Us—the most fleeting of all.
Just *once* for each thing. *Once* and no more.
And we too, just *once*. And never again. Yet to have been
this *once*, and so utterly, even if only *once*,
our having been on this *earth* can never be undone.

And so we press on and we try to achieve it,
trying with our simple hands to encompass it,
in our over-brimming gaze, in our speechless heart.
Trying to become it—who can we give it to?
We would hold on to it all forever... Ah, but what

can we carry over into that other relationship?
Not the way of seeing that has been so slowly learnt
and nothing that has happened here. Nothing.
The suffering, then. And above all, the heavy weight,
the long experience of love—just those things
that are inexpressible. But later, standing
beneath the stars, what is the use? *They* are *better*
left unspoken. For when the traveller comes
from the mountain to the valley, he brings not a handful
of the earth—inexpressible to others—but rather
a word he has won, a pure word, the yellow
and blue gentian. Perhaps we are *here* to say: house,
bridge, fountain, gate, jug, fruit tree, window—
at most: column, tower... But to *speak* them,
you understand, oh, you are to say them,
with more intensity than the things themselves
ever thought of being. Is this not the sly intent
of this secretive world when it urges lovers together—
that each thing should shudder with joy in their passion?
Threshold: what it is for two lovers, little by little,
wearing away the ancient threshold of the door,
in their turn following others who went before
and still others closing behind... gently.

Here is the time for what can be *said*—*here* its home.
Speak out and bear witness! More than ever,
things that we might experience are falling away,
are being elbowed aside and replaced by acts
without images. Acts beneath encrustations

that burst easily the moment the innards
seek out new boundaries for themselves.
Between the hammers
beats our heart, as the tongue
is still between our teeth
and still it can give praise.

Praise this world to the angel, not some
inexpressible other, because you cannot impress *him*
with sublimity in a universe where he knows
such wealth of feeling and you are a novice.
So show him something simple, something shaped
by generations, by lives like our own, near at hand,
within our sight. Tell him—things.
He will stand in amazement as you stood beside
the rope-maker in Rome, or the potter by the Nile.
Show him how happy a thing can be, how innocent,
how much ours, how even the keening of sorrow
can find its pure form and become a thing or die
into a thing, or happily outstrip itself in the violin.
And these things, which live by passing away,
as they vanish, acknowledge your praise of them,
they look to us to deliver them, we, the most
fleeting of all. They long for us to transform them,
utterly, in our invisible hearts—oh, endlessly,
to be within us—whoever, at last, we may be.

Earth, is it not this that you want: to arise
in our *invisible* sphere?—Is this not your dream,

one day to be invisible?—Earth, invisible!
What is your urgent command if it is not for
transformation? Darling earth—I will!
Oh, believe me, there is no need for the persuasion
of your springtimes—*one*, oh! a single one,
is more than my blood can take. Without a name,
I belonged to you from the start. You were always right
and your holiest inspiration is our familiar, death.

Look! I am alive! On what? Neither childhood,
nor the future is diminished... Being, in abundance,
whelms up in my heart.

The Tenth Elegy

One day, at the close of this fierce inspection—
that I might sing out in celebration and glory
to affirming angels—that none of the clear-struck
hammers of my heart might fail to sound on slack,
doubtful or broken strings—that my streaming face
be more radiant, these inconspicuous tears bloom.
Oh, then you will be dear to me, you nights
of grieving, though I did not then kneel more deeply,
more willingly in surrender, nor lose myself
in your loosened hair. How we squander our pains.
How we gaze beyond them into the miserable
distance to see if there is not, perhaps, an end.
Yet they are winter leaves, our dark evergreen,
one season of our secret year—not only a season,
but a site, settlement, camp, soil and resting place.

Of course, the byways of Grief-City are strange,
where, in the false silence born of too much noise,
swagger the plumped-up dregs from the casting
mould of emptiness: the gilded racket,
the splintering memorial. Oh, how an angel would
crush this market of consolation without trace
and the church alongside it, bought ready-made,
clean, closed, disappointing as a post office on Sunday.

Further out, the frill and flounce of the fair.
Freedom's swing-boats! Enthusiasm's jugglers
and divers! The prettified good-luck figures
from the shooting gallery that wriggle and ring
tinnily with the shot of some better marksman.
So from cheers to chancing it, he stumbles on
as stalls with all kinds of curiosities flaunt
and drum and bawl. There is—for adults only—
something special to see: how money multiplies!
in the raw! not just entertainment! money's
genitalia! the lot! the business! uncut—educational
and it will improve your performance...

       ...Oh, but just beyond that,
behind the last board plastered with posters for
Neversaydie bitter that tastes sweet to its drinkers
as long as they chew fresh distractions with it...
immediately beyond the board, right behind it,
it gets *real*. Children play there, and lovers
hold each other seriously, out of the way,
in the sparse grass, and dogs obey their nature.
The young man is drawn further on—perhaps
he is in love with a young Keening...?
Trailing her, he comes out into the meadows.
She says, 'It's far off. We live way out there...'

    'Where?' And the young man follows.
He is moved by her manner. Her shoulder—
her neck—perhaps she is of noble origin?
But he abandons her, turns about, looks back,
waves... What is the use? She is a Keening.

Only those who die young, those in their first state
of timeless serenity, still being weaned,
follow her lovingly. She waits for the girls
and befriends them, gently reveals to them
what she is wearing—her pearls of sorrow,
the fine-spun veils of patience. With young men
she walks in silence.

But out there, in the valley which they inhabit,
one of the Keening elders answers the youth
when he questions her. 'We were once a great race,'
she says to him. 'The Keening people. Our ancestors
worked the mines, up there in the mountain range.
Amongst men, sometimes you still find polished lumps
of original grief or—erupted from an ancient volcano—
a petrified clinker of rage. Yes. That came
from up there. Once, we were rich in such things…'

And gently she guides him through the vast
Keening landscape, shows him temple columns,
ruins of castles from which the Keening princes
once wisely governed the land. She shows him
the towering trees of tears, the fields of melancholy
in bloom (the living know this only in gentle leaf).
And she shows him grazing herds of mourning
and sometimes a startled bird draws far off
and scrawls flatly across their upturned gaze
and flies an image of its solitary cry. At evening,

she leads him to the graves of Keening ancestors,
the sibyls and the seers. But when night comes
they go more carefully and soon, as the moon rises,
there is a sepulchre overlooking everything,
twin brother to the one on the Nile, the tall Sphinx,
with its concealing chamber and outward
face.
And they marvel at the way the crown-like head
has forever silently positioned the human face
on the scale of the stars.

Dizzied still by his early death, the youth's eyes
can hardly grasp it. But her gaze
frightens an owl from the crown's brim and the bird brushes
slow downward strokes along the cheek—the one
with the fullest curve—and faintly,
in death's newly sharpened sense of hearing,
as on a doubled and unfolded page,
it sketches the indescribable outline.

And higher, the stars. New. Stars of the sad lands.
And slowly, the Keening names them. 'See, there,
the *Rider*, the *Staff*, and that more dense
constellation is called the *Wreath of Fruits*.
Then further up towards the Pole: *Cradle, Pathway,
the Burning Book, Puppet, Window*...
But in the southern sky, showing pure as the palm
of a blessed hand, the clear-shining *M*
that stands for Mothers...'

Yet the dead must push on, and the elder Keening
silently brings him to the foot of a ravine,
where there is, shimmering in the moonlight,
the source of joy. In reverence, she names it.
She says, 'Amongst men, this river is most buoyant.'

They stand at the foot of the mountain range.
Then she embraces him, weeping.
He climbs alone into the mountains of original grief.
And not once does his step ring on the soundless way.

*

Yet if they, these endlessly dead, woke us to comparison,
then see, perhaps they would point
to the yet-empty hazel bush, with its catkins hanging down,
or have us think of rain falling on dark soil in spring—

and we, who conceive of happiness
as something *rising*,
find in us feelings almost of dismay
when a happy thing *falls*.

FROM
SONNETS TO ORPHEUS
(1923)

I 1

There upped a tree. Oh, absolute outstripping!
Oh, Orpheus singing! Oh, tall tree in the ear!
And all things hushed. Yet even under cover
came a new start, a sign, a transforming.

From their stillness, creatures of lair and nest
pushed forwards through the clear-lit forest,
so quietly, and this—not out of cunning
and not silenced by fear—but coming

rather to listen. Bellow, shriek and roaring
shrank in their hearts. And where there stood
nothing more than a shed to receive them,

a shelter in response to their darkest need,
with its entrance, its door frame shaken,
there you built them this Temple of Hearing.

I 2

And it was a girl almost who then arose
out of this happy union of song and lyre
and gleamed clearly through her spring veils
and made herself a bed in my ear.

And slept in me. And everything was her sleep.
The trees I had always admired, even those
tangible distances, the palpable meadows,
each astonishment, all that concerned me.

She slept the world. How did you, singing God,
from the start, perfect her sleep so she had
no desire to wake? See, she arose and slept.

Where is her death? Oh, will you yet compose
on this, before your song consumes itself?
Where does she sink to, from me? ... a girl almost...

I 3

A god can do it. But tell me, how can a man
pass through the narrow lyre to follow him?
His mind is divided. At the place where two
heart-ways cross stands no Temple to Apollo.

Singing—as you teach it—is not desire,
not wooing something in the end you secure.
Singing is Being. For a god, this is easy.
But when will we *be*? And when will *he*

revolve the earth and the stars towards us?
Young man, it *is* not like love—your mouth
wrenched wide open even by that voice—

learn to forget what you once sang. It will end.
In true singing, there is a different breath.
A breath of nothing. A gust in god. A wind.

I 5

Erect no memorial stone. But let the rose
come into bloom each year on his behalf.
That is Orpheus—each metamorphosis
to this, to that. We need not struggle with

other names. Once and for all, Orpheus
is where there is singing. He comes and goes.
Is it not enough that on such occasions
for a few days he outlasts the bowl of roses?

Oh, yet he must vanish, so you comprehend!
And even though he fears this disappearing.
In this, his word outstrips our being;

already he is where you cannot follow him.
Strings of the lyre do not constrict his hands.
And he obeys just as he outplays them.

I 7

Praising, that's it! He was called to praise,
emerging from the silence of stone
like an ore. Oh, his heart—a temporary press
for man's everlasting wine.

Nor does his voice grow choked with dust,
once it is seized by the god-like example.
All becomes vineyard, all becomes juice,
in his southern land, ripe and sensual.

Even from tombs where kings have decayed,
nothing gives the lie to his praising.
Nor can the gods cause any shadow to fall.

He is the one—he is the constant herald
who, even far through the doors of the dead,
holds a bowl of fruit, ripe for the praising.

I 8

In the realm of praise only she can walk,
the Keening, nymph of the weeping spring.
She keeps close watch over our own raining,
so it tumbles clearly upon the same rock

that supports both gates and altars.
See, there, round her serene shoulders,
the dawning sense that she is youngest yet
of the brothers and sisters of the heart.

Joy *knows* and Longing merely confesses.
Only the Keening still learns all night long
on her girl's hands, telling old sadnesses.

Then suddenly—unpractised and skewed—
she raises our voices, a constellation,
high in the heaven her breath does not cloud.

I 10

Never absent from my thoughts for long,
you—I salute you, ancient sarcophagi—
through which the waters, from Roman times,
have cheerfully played their shifting song.

Or others, laid wide open as the gaze
of a herdsman as he wakes contentedly
into the rich silence of bee-drunk days,
weaving around him, delighted butterflies.

All of you—snatched away from doubt—
I salute you, your mouths gaping once more,
already knowing the meaning of silence.

Do we know it, my friends, or do we not?
Either way, it shapes the hesitant hour,
there, in the human countenance.

I 13

Pear, and plump apple, and gooseberry,
banana... all these have something to say
to the tongue, of life and death... I guess...
Read it in the expression on a child's face

as she tastes them. It comes from far off.
Slowly, does speechlessness fill your mouth?
In place of words, a flood of discovery
from the flesh of fruit, astonished, free.

Try to express what it is we call 'apple'.
This sweet one with its gathering intensity,
rising so quietly—even as you taste it—

becoming transparent, wakeful, ready,
ambiguous, sunny, earthy, native.
Oh, experience, touch, pleasure, prodigal!

I 15

Wait… that taste… it has already flown.
 …Only a little music, a stamp, a hum—
you girls, in your warmth, girls, in your silence,
dance the taste of your fruit experience!

Dance the orange. Who can forget it?
How it drowns itself in its own sweetness
while struggling against it. You possessed it.
Its transformation into you—delicious!

Dance the orange. The warmer landscape,
fling it from you, so that its ripeness
shines in our native air! Stripped, brightness,

fragrance on fragrance. Forge whatever kinship
you're able with the pure, off-putting rind,
and with the juice, brimming the lucky mind!

I 17

Ancient, tangled deeps,
all-founding root,
the hidden seeps,
never to be sought.

Helmet and hunt-horn,
grey-haired verdict,
brothers in conflict,
like lutes, their women…

Branch to branch tangled,
none of them free…
One! Oh, higher… higher…

Yet they break still.
At the very top, this only
bends to the lyre.

I 19

Though the world shifts
shape quick as clouds form,
all completed things left,
fall to their old home.

Beyond movement and change,
wider and freer,
your first song remains
still, god of the lyre.

No comprehension of hurt,
love not truly shown.
What is lost as one dies,

never really known.
Only song, above the earth,
celebrates and sanctifies.

I 20

But tell me, lord, oh what do I dedicate
to you, who taught the creatures to listen?
My memory of that one spring day,
in Russia—of a horse—in the evening…

Come from the village, a white horse alone,
round its front leg, the fetter from a stake—
freed to wander at night in the meadow,
his curling mane slapping on his neck

with the rhythms of his exuberance—
yet brutally constrained in the gallop.
How the spring of his horse-blood welled up!

He sensed the vastness—and how!
He sang and he heard it—your song sequence
utterly *in* him.

                His image: yours now.

I 21

Spring has returned again. Now the earth is
like a child who has learnt her poems by heart.
So many, so many… and for all her hard
and lengthy studies, now she takes the prize.

Her teacher was strict. How we loved the snow-
white colouring of the old man's beard.
Now we can ask her what the green is called,
the name of the blue: she knows, she knows!

Earth, you are lucky, now set free to play
with the children. We would love you to stay,
happy earth, the happiest winning out!

What the teacher taught—oh, so many things,
and all imprinted here in each root,
in the long, tangled stems—she sings, she sings!

I 22

We are the drivers.
Yet the tread of time is
a paltry thing
in the ever unchanging.

All this hurrying
will soon be passed;
for what is enduring
is our first task.

Boys, oh do not waste
your courage to race
or to fly higher.

All things are at rest:
daylight and darkness,
book and flower.

I 23

Only *then*, when flight
no more soars for itself
into the quiet skies,
thinking it is enough,

caught in bright profile,
as a device, successful,
playing the wind's darling,
slim, sure, wheeling—

only when pure enquiries
augment technology,
outdoing boyish arrogance,

will he—spurred to victory,
closing in on distance—
be what he alone flies.

I 24

The great, undemanding gods: should we disown
those old allies because they know nothing of the hard
steel we have raised up and now can discipline?
Or search a map hurriedly to see where they are?

These powerful friends who take our dead away,
yet avoid contact with our every spinning wheel:
we have stripped out banquets and places to bathe,
and their messengers now we always overhaul

because they move too slowly. But now, more lonely,
dependent on others, not knowing each other,
we drive our paths according to strict order,

no sweet meanders. Our ancient fires lit only
in steam-boilers, hoisting hammers always higher.
And yet, we are like swimmers losing power.

I 25

But it is *you* I now look for, *you*, whom I have known
like a flower, though I never guessed its name.
For them, I'll call up *once* more how you were snatched away,
beautiful playmate of the indomitable cry.

A dancer, first, then, halted suddenly, her body full
of hesitation as if her youth were cast in metal,
mournful, listening. And then, from a great height,
a music descended into her transformed heart.

Sickness was close. Shadows already taking possession,
her blood pulsed in its brief anticipation—
it darkened yet drove back towards its natural spring.

Again and again, dogged by stumbling and darkness,
it glowed, earthly, till after the terrible pounding
it stepped through the door that stood open, comfortless.

I 26

But you—singing still to the last, divine one—
even as the swarm of scorned maenads struck,
you beauty, you drowned out their shriek
with order, from ruin raised your uplifting song.

And whether they raged or wrestled, not one
could break your head, or lyre, and each sharp stone,
flung at your heart, as it touched grew softer,
gentle, and gifted with the ability to hear.

At last, they ripped you up in rash vengeance,
though your voice remained yet in rock and lion,
bird and tree. Still—you are singing there.

Oh, you lost god! You everlasting trace!
Only with the brutal scattering, your being torn,
are we listeners now and a mouth for Nature.

II 1

Breath—you invisible poem!
Forever at your pure trade
with the world's space. Counterweight. In the rhythm,
I find my place.

A singular wave,
whose sea, gradually, I become;
the thriftiest of all kinds of ocean—
accumulating space.

And of these regions of space, how many were stored
within me already? Many a wind
strikes me as a son.

Do you know me, air, full of places once mine?
You—once the smooth rind,
the rounding-out and leaf of my every word.

II 2

As sometimes, the master's *genuine* stroke
will find the nearest, hurried page;
so often, in the same way, a mirror will take
to itself the smiling, sacred, unique face

of a girl as she tries on the morning alone,
or sits in the lamplight's flattering gleam.
And before the breath of faces more real,
later, she lets slip only a counterfeit glow.

What did we once glimpse with our eyes,
staring at the hearth, its slow-burning coal?
Visions of life—forever lost to us.

Oh, earth, who can number your losses?
None—or only the one who still sounds praise,
singing his heart out, born to the whole.

II 5

Flower-muscle that opens the anemone
in its meadow-mornings, step by step,
until the noisy polyphony
of heaven pours its light into her lap,

into the rapt, quiet, star-flower's shape,
its muscle's endless receptivity,
at times, overwhelmed by *such* bounty,
until, come the signal of declining day,

there is hardly enough strength to retrieve
the petals' edges, they are so unfurled:
you, power and will of *how* many worlds!

We, though brutal-born, far longer survive,
and yet, *when*, in which of all our lives,
will we be ever open, will we receive?

II 6

You, enthroned rose, to those in ancient time
you were a simple cup with a plain rim.
But for *us*, you are the full bloom,
the countless, the inexhaustible thing.

In your wealth, you are like layer on layer,
round a body composed of nothing but light;
yet your single petal seems to declare
the shunning, the denial of such attire.

For centuries, your odour has called out
its sweetest names to us—
suddenly, it hangs like fame in the air.

Still, we do not know what to call it—we guess...
And memory sets out to recover it
and goes begging every acquiescent hour.

II 7

Flowers—kin to arranging hands at last
(hands of girls from the present and the past),
laid edge to edge on a table in a garden,
quite exhausted from the gentle wounding,

waiting for the water that will serve to pull
you away from death's beginning. Once more,
lifted now between the streaming pole
of each sensitive finger, possessed of a power

to help you, light ones, more than you can guess,
you recover now, gradually, in the vase—
cooling, giving up the warmth of those girls,

as if confessing a weary and tedious sin,
committed in being picked—and yet, still kin
to them, in their flowering, allies of yours.

II 10

All we have achieved, threatened by machinery
if it dares to live for itself rather than obey.
The craftsman's fine, tentative hand gone:
stone cut more stiffly for its stark construction.

It never holds back, so we might *once* break free,
oiling itself for itself in a workplace without noise.
It is life—it believes in its own ability,
with equal resolve, orders, creates, destroys.

Yet life remains enchanted for us. See it rouse
from a hundred places—the play of pure power
that none feels without kneeling to admire.

Delicate still, words reach for the unsayable…
And music, always new, in a space unworkable,
from trembling stones builds its divine house.

II 11

Since you insist on hunting, all-conquering man,
many orderly, calm rules have risen round death.
I know you better than a trap or net, you strip of sailcloth,
they would hang far down into the Karst cavern.

They lowered you softly, as if you were a symbol,
a mark of peace. A boy seized an edge, gave it a shake,
and night flung a handful of white doves from the cave,
reeling into the light… And even *that* is lawful.

Those watching remain far from any touch of pity,
not just the hunter, who quickly proves himself,
playing his part, always primed and ready.

To kill is one form of our restless grief…
The serene spirit lives pure—
whatever it is we have to endure.

II 12

Seek transformation. Oh, be eager for that flame
in which something escapes you, proud of change.
In overcoming the earthbound, that designing spirit
loves the zest of a figure at its turning point.

Whatever locks itself shut *has* already petrified.
Does it feel safe and secure in inconspicuous grey?
Wait—the hard warned by the hardest far away.
Woe betide—a distant hammer lifted high!

Whoever pours himself like a spring, realization
realizes him, leading him, joyful, to calm creation,
which in opening closes, often ceases by starting.

Each happy place is a child or grandchild of parting,
passed in amazement. And Daphne, transformed,
in feeling herself laurel, wants you changed to wind.

II 13

Anticipate all parting—as if it were
behind you already, like the winter passed by.
For beneath winters lies one infinite winter,
and only by wintering out can your heart survive.

Be forever dead in Eurydice—by singing ascend,
and give praise, rise into the pure relation.
Here, amongst fading things, in a realm of decline,
be a ringing glass shattered by its own sound.

Be—and know the state of Not-Being too,
that infinite source of your innermost vibration—
so you carry it, this once, to completion.

To the used-up—to all Nature's musty and mute,
its brimming storehouse, its inexpressible sum—
joyously add yourself and the account's done.

II 15

Oh, fountain-mouth, you voice, you giver—
of purity, and inexhaustible oneness, you speak.
Set before the face of the flowing water,
you are a marble mask. And further back,

the source of the aqueducts: from far-off hills
of the Apennines, flowing past graves,
they bring down to you a speech that spills
over your chin, where it blackens with age,

until, into the vessel before you, it falls.
This is the ear, laid out, fast asleep,
the marble ear, into which you always speak.

The ear of earth. And so it is, she calls
only to herself alone. Push in to fill a pitcher,
and she feels as if you have interrupted her.

II 17

Where—in what watered, ever-blessed gardens,
in what tree, what tenderly stripped calyx—ripens
the exotic fruit of consolation? You might find
one of these delicacies in the trampled field

of your poverty. There will be times you marvel
at the size of the fruit, that it remains whole,
at the softness of the skin, that the thoughtlessness
of birds has not already taken it, nor the jealous

worms from below. Are there trees dressed by angels?
Are there obscure, slow-moving gardeners at work
to bring us crops that are not really ours?

Have we—shadows and spectres—never been able,
in our hurrying to ripen and as quickly wither back,
to disturb the balance of these calm summers?

II 18

Dancer: oh, you translation
of fading things into movement. How you showed us!
And that last pirouette, that tree of motion,
did it not take possession of the year spinning past?

From stillness, did the treetop not suddenly bloom,
where before your whirling swarmed round it in flight?
And above, was it not sun, and summer, and heat—
incalculable heat, kindled by you?

Yet it bore too, it bore, your ecstatic tree.
Are these not its peaceful fruit: this striped pitcher,
where it ripens, and this vase, grown even riper?

And in the pictures, does the image not remain
of your eyebrow's dark streak,
rapidly scrawled across the wall of your spin?

II 19

In the pampered banks somewhere, gold is alive
and a friend to thousands. Yet this beggar,
this blind man, he, even to a copper coin, is like
a lost place under a cupboard, a dusty corner.

All round the shops, money is perfectly at ease
and seems to disguise itself in flowers, fur and silk.
The silent one, he stands in the breathing space
of money's breath, where all things sleep or wake.

How does it close at night, the hand, forever open?
Come morning, again, fate takes it up, each day
holds it out, pale, wretched, always close to ruin.

If only, amazed at last, one might see, grasp and praise
this long endurance. Only in singing might it be said.
Only ever heard by the god.

II 21

My heart, sing gardens, though you do not know them,
clear and unreachable, as if fixed under glass.
Water and roses from Ispahan or Shiraz—
praise them, sing their bliss, beyond comparison.

Show, my heart, you cannot live without them,
that they have thoughts of you—their ripening figs—
and, passing amongst their flowering sprigs,
you are like a breeze on the face of a loved one.

Do not make this mistake: that deprivation is due
to a decision you made—this one: to be!
In the weave, you are silken thread sewn through.

In you—whatever other dear image is present
(even if an instant from this life of agony),
know this, the whole glorious carpet is meant.

II 23

Then call on me at that hour of your day
that continually offers resistance:
like the face of a dog, imploring and up close,
over and over, forever turning away,

just when you think you have grasped it at last.
What is withdrawn in this way is most your own.
We are free. We were dismissed,
just when we thought we were sure of welcome.

Anxiously, we seek a firm hold,
yet sometimes we are too young for what is old,
and too old for what has never been.

Still, we do justice only when we give praise,
since we are ah! the branch, and we are the blade,
and the sweetness of ripening jeopardy.

II 25

Listen, the first ploughs are already at work.
Once again, hear the human rhythm
in the measured stillness of the strong earth
in early spring. For you, what is to come

does not appear stale. And what so often
seemed a repetition of the past, like new
now returns. Always, in anticipation,
although you never seized it. It seized you.

Even oak leaves that outlast the winter,
though lit brown in the evening: the future.
And occasionally, signals on the breeze.

The bushes are black. Yet heaps of manure,
spread, even richer black, over the meadows.
And, as each hour passes, it grows younger.

II 26

How we are shaken by the shriek of a bird…
By any cry that is uniquely conjured.
Yet children, playing under open skies,
are already yelling above the genuine cry.

They call at random. Into the heart of space,
into intervals (in which, all of a piece,
the bird's cry passes like people in dreams)
like wedges, they drive home their screams.

Oh, where are we? Always, ever freer,
like kites ripped away from their mooring string,
edges shredded in a gale, now chattering,

we flutter in mid-air. Marshal every crier,
you singing god, so their awakening is a roar,
like a torrent bearing the head and the lyre.

II 28

Oh, come and gone. You, still a child almost,
to the empty constellation supply a figure
of dance, in which for a moment we surpass,
if only briefly, the dulled order of Nature.

Because she, herself, was only truly excited
when she heard Orpheus, when he first sang.
Since then, you have been moved by it,
and a little confused, when a tree took so long

to choose to go with you, where you listen.
You have always known the place where the lyre
was lifted, ringing, the unheard-of core.

For this, you tried out your beautiful steps,
in hope of turning your friend, his face, perhaps,
his course, one day, towards healing celebration.

II 29

Silent friend of many distances, now feel
how space increases even as you breathe.
From the wooden beams of a dark belfry,
ring yourself out loud. For whatever feeds

on you gains strength from such sustenance.
Travel always towards transformation.
What has been your most painful experience?
If the draught tastes bitter, turn it to wine.

In this night of excess, you must perform
magic at the crossroads of your senses—show
the meaning of their strange encounter.

And if all that is earthly knows you no more,
declare this to the stilled world: I flow.
And say this to the rushing waters: I am.

LAST POEMS (1923–1926)
FROM
THE VALAISIAN QUATRAINS

1 *Little Fountain*

Nymph, ever draping yourself
in what strips you bare,
let your body exalt itself
for the waves' smack and stir.

Tirelessly changing clothes
and your hair's appearance;
your life, beyond such loss,
remains pure presence.

2

Landscape, paused halfway between
earth and blue heaven:
voices of bronze and waters ring,
tender, tough, old and young,

like an offering lifted up
to grateful hands outspread:
beautiful, achieved landscape,
warm as bread!

5

Gentle curve beside the ivy,
side track where goats roam;
jewellers, loving this light,
would wrap its beauty in stone.

Poplar, in its proper place:
its vertical as counterpoint
to slow verdure's vigorous
sprawl and stretching out.

6

Silent land, your prophets hushed still,
            region readying its wine;
the scent of Genesis yet on every hill
            and no fear of what is to come!

Country, too proud to crave what transforms,
            which—obeying summertime—
appears, like the walnut trees and the elms,
            content to repeat again.

Whose waters are almost the sole new thing,
            waters, giving themselves at once,
everywhere, their clear vowels ringing,
            in the midst of your hard consonants!

7

See, high meadows fit for an angel,
        amongst the dark pines, up there?
In the uncanny light, they appear more
        than distant, almost celestial.

Yet from bright valley to high summit,
        what ethereal treasures shine!
All that floats in the air, reflected in it,
        will pass into your wine.

11

Let's still bring to this sacred place
all that feeds us: the fruit of the vine,
bread and salt, and so let's amaze
the mother with this vast maternal realm.

This chapel, down through the ages,
binds ancient deity to future god,
and this old walnut tree, this tree-magus,
like a pure temple, offers its shade.

17

Before you count to ten,
all's changed: the breeze
snatches this light from
the tall stalks of maize,

only to let it drop,
where it flits and glides
along an outcrop
towards a sister-light,

which, already, in turn,
playing her part
in this roughhouse game,
shifts to a new height.

As if—beneath a caress—
the vast land remains
dazzled by gestures
that perhaps gave it shape.

18

Trail that winds and plays
amongst the slanting vines,
like a ribbon someone ties
round a hat on summer days.

Vine: you sport the bonnet,
wine engendering there.
Wine: a fiery comet,
promise to the coming year.

21

After a day full of gales,
in a peace to last forever,
eventually evening settles
like a compliant lover.

All becomes clear, calm...
Yet glowing, golden-streaked,
piled on the horizon,
clouds in lovely bas-relief.

25

Down the length of this dusty way,
the green takes on a greyish hue,
but a grey—if only faintly—
touched with silver and blue.

Elsewhere, on higher ground,
a willow flaunts the sheen
beneath its leaves to the wind,
before a black that is close to green.

Nearby, a quite abstract green,
the pale green of vision,
wraps in depths of dereliction
the tower the century is undoing.

26

Proud decline of these towers
that still can remember—
from who knows when to forever—
their lives passed in the air.

This incalculable relation
with the penetrating light,
renders them slow to motion
and their decay more acute.

28

Country that sings while labouring,
a land content in its work;
while the waters go on with their singing,
the vines forge link on link.

Hushed land, for the song of the waters
is simply excess of silence—
the silence that falls between words
as, rhythmically, they advance.

31

Paths that lead to nowhere,
crossing this or that meadow,
seeming to take great care
not to reach where they might go.

Paths that oftentimes have
nothing laid out before them,
but pure expanse
and the season.

35

The earth converses here
with the attentive heavens;
memory overwhelms her
amongst these noble mountains.

Sometimes she seems surprised
that we listen so well—
then she reveals her whole life
and has no more to tell.

36

Near the ground, a butterfly
displays the illuminations
of its lovely book of flight
for Nature's admiration.

On a sweet-smelling flower,
another is closing its leaves:
this is no time to read.
Then others, so many more,

of tiny blues, at a glance,
rising, they float, they spin
like the pallid blue scraps
of a love letter in the wind,

a letter torn to pieces,
yet written moments before,
while the one intended to read it
hesitated at the door.

NOTES ON SOME OF THE POEMS

pages 29–55:—*The Book of Monastic Life* (1899), *The Book of Pilgrimage* (1901) and *The Book of Poverty and Death* (1903) were collected in 1905 as *The Book of Hours*. There, the untitled poems, from each of the three original books, were presented as three unbroken sequences as if a series of prayers or spiritual exercises. In this selection, I indicate breaks introduced into Rilke's original sequence with [...], whereas poems that run on from each other, as they did in *The Book of Hours*, are here separated by *.

page 54: 'Oh, where is he, the one whose power rose'—St Francis.

page 74: 'Those of the House of Colonna'—the House of Colonna is an aristocratic Italian family. Part of the papal nobility, its members played a significant role in the history and political life of Rome between the twelfth and sixteenth centuries.

page 88: 'Roman Sarcophagi'—these ancient Roman stone coffins, later emptied and used as conduits for water, fascinated Rilke. The Greek origins of the word mean 'flesh-eating', and these are the poem's 'unknown mouths'.

page 98: 'Tombs of the Hetaerae'—the hetaerae were courtesans in ancient Greece. Often highly educated, as well as providing sexual services they performed roles as artists, entertainers and conversationalists.

page 100: 'Orpheus. Eurydice. Hermes.'—Orpheus is the musician who sings and plays so beautifully that even animals, rocks and trees are irresistibly drawn to his music. He falls in love with the nymph Eurydice but, bitten by a snake, she dies, and the grieving Orpheus goes to the underworld to recover her. His playing enchants even Hades and Persephone, who allow him to return with Eurydice, accompanied by Hermes, on one condition: he must not look back till they have both reached the land of the living. Nearing the surface, Orpheus is so overjoyed that he looks back and Eurydice returns to the underworld forever. As alluded to in Rilke's later *Sonnets to Orpheus*, the musician/artist spends the rest of his life grieving for Eurydice, but this infuriates the Maenads, a group of women who worship the god Dionysus. Probably to punish Orpheus for neglecting their attentions, they tear him to pieces, throwing his head and lyre into the River Hebrus. His head continues to sing, and the lyre continues to play. Eventually, the gods place the lyre in the heavens as a constellation.

page 163: 'First Duino Elegy'—Gaspara Stampa (1523–54) was an Italian noblewoman and poet who wrote of her love of, and rejection by, Count Collatino di Collalto in a series of 311 sonnets.

page 165: 'First Duino Elegy'—Linus is referred to in *The Iliad*, Book 18. In one version of his story, Linus is a poet who dies young and is mourned by Apollo. It is the provocation of his death that first caused music to fill the wilderness.

page 166: 'Second Duino Elegy'—Tobias is referred to in the apocryphal Book of Tobit. He is unwittingly accompanied on a journey by the angel Raphael.

page 175: 'Fifth Duino Elegy'—'the capital D of Destiny' is an allusion to Picasso's 1905 painting *La Famille des Saltimbanques*, which Rilke saw in 1914. The five standing figures in the painting, adults and children, appear to be arranged in the shape of a capital D.

page 197: *Sonnets to Orpheus*—above Rilke's desk at Muzot, in 1921, hung a reproduction of Cima da Conegliano's pen and ink drawing (*c*.1500) of Orpheus singing and playing to the assembled creatures.